A movement outside caught Hawk's attention. The men had found the cabin.

"We need to go. Get your coats, leave the duffel behind. We're heading out the back."

"The back?" The confusion in Jillian's green gaze morphed into fear. "They're here?"

He nodded. Keeping Jillian in front of him, he covered their backs as he guided them into the woods. Hawk continued sweeping his gaze over the area, looking for signs the hostiles were near.

When they reached the cluster of bushes, he carved out a small space with his hands and drew Jillian down. "Stay here. I'll be back soon."

She clutched at his arm. "Don't leave us," she begged.

"I have a snowmobile nearby. I promise I'll be quick."

Tears welled in her eyes, but she gave a jerky nod, showing she understood. He drew out his gun and handed it to her.

He hesitated. There was so much he wanted to say, but there wasn't time. He needed to move, to draw the hostiles away from Jillian and Lizzy.

He'd willingly sacrifice himself to keep them alive and safe.

Laura Scott is a nurse by day and an author by night. She has always loved romance and read faith-based books by Grace Livingston Hill in her teenage years. She's thrilled to have published over twenty-five books for Love Inspired Suspense. She has two adult children and lives in Milwaukee, Wisconsin, with her husband of over thirty years. Please visit Laura at laurascottbooks.com, as she loves to hear from her readers.

Books by Laura Scott

Love Inspired Suspense

Justice Seekers

Soldier's Christmas Secrets

Callahan Confidential

Shielding His Christmas Witness
The Only Witness
Christmas Amnesia
Shattered Lullaby
Primary Suspect
Protecting His Secret Son

True Blue K-9 Unit

Blind Trust

Military K-9 Unit

Battle Tested
Military K-9 Unit Christmas
"Yuletide Target"

Visit the Author Profile page at Harlequin.com for more titles.

SOLDIER'S CHRISTMAS SECRETS

LAURA SCOTT

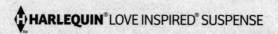
HARLEQUIN® LOVE INSPIRED® SUSPENSE

Recycling programs
for this product may
not exist in your area.

LOVE INSPIRED BOOKS

ISBN-13: 978-1-335-23244-1

Soldier's Christmas Secrets

www.Harlequin.com

Printed in U.S.A.

Be strong and of a good courage, fear not, nor be afraid of them: for the Lord thy God, he it is that doth go with thee; he will not fail thee, nor forsake thee.
–Deuteronomy 31:6

This book is dedicated to Michael Christman, a man who has bravely faced cancer only to come out stronger within his faith. This book is for you.

ONE

Hawk Jacobson parked his SUV and moved silently through the dark, cold December night, automatically raking his gaze over the area searching for a possible threat. As a private investigator, he didn't have set hours, and tonight he was returning home later than usual.

After entering his house, he didn't bother turning his lights on as he made his way through the interior. Hawk paused near the side window, the one overlooking Jillian's home. Dark windows outlined by bright Christmas lights indicated his neighbor, Jillian Wade, and her young daughter, Lizzy, had retired for the night.

Just as he was about to step back from the window, he saw two men, dressed in black from head to toe, ski masks covering their faces and guns held at the ready in their hands, moving silently through the night and heading straight for Jillian's house. *No!* Hawk sprang into action. Armed with a knife and a gun, yet hoping not to use either, he silently let himself out of his house. Picking the second man who was still standing on the driveway as his target, he stealthily approached from behind. With surprise on his side, he took him down, hitting him in the back of the head and rendering him unconscious. With one hostile out of commission, he went searching for the other.

The front door of Jillian's house was ajar, and he hated knowing the guy had breached her personal space. Years of military training enabled Hawk to move silently down the hall. The gunman was hovering between the two bedroom doorways, as if unsure which one to try first. Indecision was his enemy. Hawk grabbed him from behind, covered the guy's mouth and took him roughly to the ground and held his gun at his temple.

"Who sent you?" Hawk asked in a harsh whisper. "Why are you here?"

The man's eyes, which Hawk could see from the round openings of the ski mask, showed no emotion. The hostile didn't make a sound, apparently too well-trained to talk. Hawk was about to knock the guy unconscious when a slight movement caught his eye. The door to the second bedroom was open a crack and he saw Lizzy's frightened face peering out at him.

He froze, wishing more than anything that the little girl didn't look so terrified. Was she afraid of the gun? Probably, but he couldn't risk hiding it from her. "It's okay," he called softly. "It's me. Hawk."

She quickly closed the door. With a frustrated sigh, Hawk pressed on the man's twin carotid arteries to put him to sleep, making sure he was unconscious but not dead. He took a moment to lift the ski mask, but the man's face wasn't familiar. Hawk didn't recognize him. Leaving him be, Hawk rose to his feet and lightly rapped on Jillian's door. "Jillian? It's Hawk. I'm coming in."

"Hawk?" Jillian's voice was sleepy. "What are you doing here?"

Entering her room felt wrong, but there wasn't a moment to waste. The two hostiles wouldn't stay unconscious forever. "I stopped two guys from trying to kill you. Get up. We need to leave."

"What are you talking about?" She sounded grumpy. "What two men? I can't leave. Lizzy's asleep."

"No, she's not. I just saw her. One man is on the driveway near the front door, the other is just outside your room. Hurry. I'll get Lizzy while you throw some stuff together. But don't pack like this is a vacation, we're traveling light."

"But…"

Hawk was done talking. He turned and made his way to Lizzy's room, stepping carefully over the body on the floor. He pressed again on the guy's neck to give them more time, then reached for the door of the second bedroom and opened it. "Lizzy? It's Hawk. I know you're scared, but you and your mom need to come with me, okay?"

Lizzy didn't answer. Not that he really expected her to. He stood for a moment, sweeping his gaze over the area. Lizzy's bed was empty. There was a small desk, a dollhouse, a closet and dresser. She must be hiding in fear, likely in the closet or under the bed.

The bed. He dropped to his hands and knees, pressed his cheek to the floor. "Lizzy, your mom is waiting for us. We need to go."

A muffled sob was the only sound she uttered.

His heart squeezed painfully in his chest, but he forced himself to ignore it. There was no time to waste. He reached under the twin bed, found her arm and tugged. She resisted, but the little girl was no match for him. He gently pulled her out and gathered her stiff body into his arms. She clutched a tattered brown teddy bear against her pink fleece footie pajamas, like a shield.

"I'm sorry, Lizzy. But we have to go." He carried her to the next room, where a grim-faced Jillian was dressed in jeans and a sweatshirt, tossing items into an overnight duffel bag.

"Lizzy." She held out her arms for her daughter and Lizzy practically jumped to get away from him, grabbing onto her mother and clinging like a baby monkey.

He told himself not to take it personally as he slung the duffel over his shoulder and cupped Jillian's elbow in his hand. "Grab coats for you and Lizzy. We'll take my car."

"I'm not sure—" She stopped abruptly when she saw the man lying in the hallway. "Who? What? Oh my—" She looked as if she might scream, so he cut her off.

"Later. We need to be quiet in case there are others nearby." Hawk steered her around the body. The man groaned, indicating they were running out of time.

In the kitchen, Jillian snagged her purse from the counter. They paused long enough to grab winter gear, especially for Lizzy. There hadn't been time to change her out of her pajamas, but that didn't stop Jillian from putting winter boots on her daughter. Hawk waited impatiently, desperate to get them out of the house.

Outside, the second man remained unmoving. Hawk's SUV was in the driveway, where he'd left it. But Jillian dug in her heels, resisting him much like her daughter.

"Wait. Where are we going? Shouldn't we call the police? I don't understand…"

"Not now," he said forcefully. "We'll talk later."

"Fine, but I'm not going without Lizzy's car seat."

Giving in was easier than arguing. "Give me your keys, then get into the SUV."

Thankfully she did as she was told. He grabbed the child seat out of Jillian's rusted sedan and hurried over to his vehicle. Within minutes he had the car seat strapped in and Lizzy plunked inside. The little girl's crying shredded him.

After sliding in behind the wheel, he wasted no time in backing out of the driveway. Keeping an eye on Jillian's house in the rearview mirror as he drove away, he caught a fleeting glimpse of a black-clad man staggering out through the front door, holding the ski mask in his hand.

Fearing more hostiles on the way, Hawk hit the gas, speeding as fast as he dared through the slick, snow-covered streets of their Brookland, Wisconsin, neighborhood, until he reached Highway 18. Then he headed west toward the interstate.

"I don't understand," Jillian said. "What's going on? Who were those men?"

He glanced over at her. "I don't know. But they were armed and dangerous."

"Why did they come after me?" Jillian's voice sounded shaky and confused. He had to give her credit for not falling apart. She lifted a hand to her long, dark-red hair, a gold wedding band on the third finger of her left hand glinting in the moonlight.

"Could they have been looking for your husband?"

"My husband is dead," she said in a flat tone.

"Lizzy's father?"

She glared at him with clear exasperation. "Weren't you listening? My husband, Lizzy's father, is dead. James was killed in Afghanistan a few years ago."

Hawk went perfectly still, his gaze locked on the highway stretching out before him. He wanted to tell Jillian that he was really James—and that he wasn't dead. That he didn't die in Afghanistan but almost had from a small plane crash that had killed his three teammates and their pilot, deep in the Appalachian Mountains. That despite the fact that he looked completely different thanks to the horrible facial fractures and scars he now wore on his face, he was right here, next to her. But the words remained locked in his throat.

Two hostiles. Professional hit men. No way they had shown up just to take out Jillian or Lizzy.

They'd come for him.

To finish the job of killing him.

Jillian gripped the armrest with such force her fingertips went numb. Two men wearing ski masks and carrying guns had come to her house! She couldn't comprehend what was happening—it was all so surreal. If she hadn't seen them for herself, one lying in the hallway and the other on the snow-covered ground, she would have thought Hawk had lost his mind.

Lizzy's crying increased in volume.

"It's okay, Lizzy." She reached back to stroke her daughter's knee. The four-year-old was obviously terrified. "We're fine, see? Everything is just fine. Mr. Hawk has come to save us, isn't that nice? We're going to be all right."

It took a while, but her daughter's sobs slowly quieted. As Jillian had hoped, the little girl began to nod off, still clutching the teddy bear close. Car rides had that effect on her.

Jillian glanced at Hawk. Her strong, silent, scarred yet kind neighbor who didn't say much but was always there to lend a hand. At times it was as if he knew what she needed done before she did. She would come home from work to find her lawn had been mowed or a broken shutter repaired. Just that morning he'd gotten up early to shovel her driveway so that it was clear before she needed to head to work, the last day of school before Christmas break. It was odd yet sweet. Hawk wasn't one for small talk, either. He would simply lift a hand to acknowledge her, and that was all.

Frankly they'd spoken more tonight than they had in the five months she'd known him.

She was grateful he was there to help her now. She noticed Hawk kept his eyes on the road and made several turns, getting off the interstate, taking side streets and then getting back on. He was obviously taking care to be sure they weren't followed.

Not once since he'd moved in next door had he ever made her feel uncomfortable. He'd never indicated he was interested in anything other than being neighborly. Maybe because he assumed she was married.

Her gaze dropped to the gold wedding band her deceased husband had given to her five years ago. She'd taken the diamond engagement ring off but not the plain band. She wasn't sure why. James had been the love of her life, but barely a year after they'd married he was deployed to Afghanistan. Two months after he'd gotten there, he'd been sent off on some secret mission that he couldn't talk about. One that had ultimately killed him.

James had never known about Lizzy. She hadn't known about her pregnancy until after he'd died. She'd never understood why God had taken James from her so quickly, and she had stopped attending church after his death for several months. When she'd moved here to be closer to her mother, she'd found her faith and comfort in the church again.

"Jillian?"

"Huh?" She pulled away from her sorrowful thoughts. "I'm sorry, what did you say?"

"I have a cabin in the north woods. I'd like to take you and Lizzy there until we can figure out what's going on."

"A cabin?" She wasn't sure why the news surprised her. In the months she'd known Hawk, he'd been home at odd hours. Sometimes leaving before she did, and at other times, remaining at home as she left for school. In fact she'd often wondered exactly what he did for work but hadn't wanted to pry. From the scar on his face, she thought he might be on disability or something. He knew she was a second grade school teacher at Brookland Elementary, but only because she'd offered the information.

"I don't want you to feel uncomfortable with me," he went on. "There are two bedrooms, a small kitchen and bathroom with indoor plumbing. It will be safer there than at a motel."

"Safer how? I still can't figure out why those two men came to find me in the first place. I'm a teacher. Why would anyone want to hurt me?"

"I know. I'm sorry."

She let out a sigh. None of this was his fault. "Your cabin sounds fine. But shouldn't we call the police?"

"Not yet."

She frowned. "Why not?"

"By the time the police arrive, the two gunmen will be long gone. I only temporarily incapacitated them, I didn't kill them. There's no real proof of what happened—it would be our word against no one. I need to do a little digging before we call the authorities."

She wasn't sure she understood his rationale, but the idea that the gunmen might already be gone bothered her. She wished she'd thought to take a picture with her cell phone, especially of the guy lying on the floor outside her bedroom.

Silence stretched between them. Now that Lizzy was asleep, her thoughts raced. One gunman had gotten all the way inside her house. How was it that she hadn't heard anything? She was normally an extremely light sleeper.

And how had Hawk gotten there in time to prevent the gunmen from hurting her? The fact that he'd taken out two gunmen without making a sound should have scared her to death.

But she felt safe. Ironic, since she didn't even know Hawk's last name or what he did for a living.

"Hawk—is that your real name?"

"Yes." He cleared his throat. "Hawk Jacobson."

She nodded, rolling the name around in her mind. "I want to thank you. For coming over to save us."

He was silent for a long moment. "I'm just glad I was able to get to you and Lizzy in time."

"Me, too." She shivered and rubbed her hands together. "How far is the cabin?"

"Thirty minutes." He glanced at her, his gaze impossible to read in the darkness. "Try to get some rest."

She shook her head, knowing sleep would be impossible. "Do you think this could be related to one of my students? Like maybe one of the kids' parents is into something illegal? I just can't figure out what else it could be."

"Anything is possible." Hawk's voice was husky and a bit hoarse, something she hadn't noticed before now.

As if he might have a sore throat. "When we get to the cabin you can make a list of possible suspects."

"They're students, not suspects." The words were sharp and she winced, knowing she was taking her frustration out on Hawk. "Besides, I think the police should be the one to search for the men responsible."

Another brief pause before Hawk spoke. "I'm a private investigator and I have friends who are cops in the Milwaukee Police Department. I need you to trust my judgment on this. Give me a little time to figure out what's going on."

Hawk Jacobson. Private Investigator. Friends who were cops. That was a whole lot more than she'd known about him an hour ago.

"Okay," she reluctantly agreed.

The rest of the car ride was silent. Hawk exited the freeway and took a curvy highway heading northwest. Then he pulled off on the side of the road and shut down the vehicle.

"I need to go in on foot, make sure the place is safe," he told her. He took a gun out of his side holster and held it out to her. "Stay here. If anyone approaches, I want you to shoot first and ask questions later."

She recoiled from the weapon as if it were a venomous snake. "I'm not touching that thing." She glanced at Lizzy. "We're better off without it."

Hawk's lips tightened, giving her the impression he wasn't happy. But he so rarely revealed any emotion that she thought she may have misinterpreted it. He gently placed the weapon in her lap. "You'll use it if your life or Lizzy's is threatened."

Without waiting for her to respond, he slipped out of the car and shut the door behind him.

She watched him round the front of the SUV and head into the woods. One minute he was there, the next he was gone, somehow without leaving obvious boot prints in the snow behind. The man moved with incredible silence, making her wonder where he'd learned such a skill.

The service? Had Hawk spent time in the military the way James had? Yet if that was the case, why was he working as a private investigator? Why not join a police force?

She shook her head. This insatiable curiosity about her neighbor wasn't healthy. Hawk's personal decisions were not any of her business. She wasn't interested in anything beyond friendship.

Ignoring the gun in her lap, she twisted the wedding band on her finger, thinking about James. How much she missed him. How he was everything she could have asked for in a husband and how he would have been an amazing father to Lizzy.

Then she thought about Hawk. Who was here, now. Who had not only helped her with house maintenance without being asked but was determined to keep her and Lizzy safe.

She slipped the ring off, and then, besieged by a rush of guilt, pushed it back on. Staring out through the windshield, she wondered how long it would take Hawk to check out the cabin. This sitting in the darkness, waiting, was getting on her nerves.

She heard a noise and froze. Then she did something she never thought she'd do. She picked up the gun. It felt heavy and cold in her hand and she had to wrap both her hands around the handle to keep it steady.

Another rustle and she instinctively knew the sound wasn't from Hawk returning. The man was too quiet to cause this much noise. She tightened her grip on the gun, sweeping her gaze from the windshield to the passenger-side window, searching for anything amiss.

Two deer walked out from the woods. They stopped, looked at her with glassy eyes and then gracefully leaped and ran across the street right in front of the SUV.

She let out her breath in a whoosh. Deer. A doe and her fawn. Not men wearing ski masks.

Yet she didn't release her grip on the gun.

Five minutes later, she noticed a dark shadow stepping out of the woods. She tightened her grip on the weapon but within a few seconds recognized the shadow as Hawk. The moonlight on his face made it easy to see his scar.

He quietly approached the car, nodding an acknowledgement when he caught her looking at him. He came around and slid into the driver's seat.

"It's clear."

She held out the weapon. "Take this. I don't want it."

He took the gun and pushed it back into its holster. He drove a quarter mile down the road and turned into a gravel driveway.

The cabin was about a hundred yards in, nicely surrounded by trees. He pulled to a stop and then climbed out. "Do you want me to carry Lizzy?"

"I'll get her. She might cry if she wakes up to a stranger."

He nodded, grabbed the duffel and went over to hold the door. A dusting of snow clung to her boots, so she kicked the lower doorjamb to clear them before going inside. Lizzy snuggled against her chest as Jillian carried her across the living room. She hesitated, glancing at Hawk questioningly.

"There are twin beds in this room." He opened the door to the right of what looked to be a bathroom. "The other room is off the kitchen."

"Thanks." She went inside and gently set Lizzy on the twin bed closest to the door. After removing her winter coat and boots, she tucked her daughter into the sleeping bag on top of the bed. She straightened and turned to find Hawk standing close.

Too close.

In the darkness she couldn't see his face very clearly, but she had often wondered about the deep scar he carried along his left cheek. Catching a whiff of his aftershave, she found her pulse kicking up and her knees going weak.

It was the same brand James used to buy.

"Excuse me." Moving abruptly, she ducked around him and left the bedroom. Her heart was pounding erratically and for a moment she feared she was losing her mind.

In that brief instant, she'd thought the man standing beside her was James. Same height, same weight, same aftershave.

Impossible. James was dead. This was nothing more than her overactive imagination playing tricks on her. Hormones reacting to a familiar scent.

She wasn't interested in a relationship with Hawk.

Yet for the moment, her life and Lizzy's depended on him. On his strength and ability to keep them both safe from harm.

TWO

Battling guilt, Hawk silently followed Jillian into the living room and began making a fire in the wood-burning stove to heat up the cabin. He hadn't meant to frighten her, but given the way she'd bolted out of the room, he knew he must have. He'd worked hard over the past several months to remain nonthreatening. To provide help without getting too close.

But discovering Lizzy was his daughter had changed things. He'd wanted to peer down at her tiny face while she slept. He'd wanted the right to bend down to kiss her forehead and whisper good-night.

Unfortunately, his life, the life he should have had, remained far out of reach. Maybe forever.

Not that it should matter. There were more important things to worry about at the moment. Like who'd sent professional assassins to Jillian's home. To kidnap them? Or kill them? Kidnapping he could understand, because it would be a way to use Jillian and Lizzy as leverage against him. But killing them made no sense.

It occurred to him that if his real identity had been uncovered, then the assassins would have come directly to his house, not Jillian's. Which meant his current identity was safe.

For now.

Yet he knew his recent probing into Rick Barton's past had not gone unnoticed. Senator Barton was a powerful man in Washington, DC, but very few knew the truth about how Barton had climbed the ranks. Hawk must have gotten close enough to discover certain information about Barton to trip someone's suspicions.

Almost two years had passed since he'd begun to remember his past, yet it also felt as if it had only happened yesterday. His memory had more holes in it than Swiss cheese. He hadn't even remembered Jillian right away. Memories and images had come to him in bits and pieces.

He was the only special ops soldier who knew the truth about what happened in Afghanistan, and even then, he didn't have a good memory to guide him. The other members of his team who'd been with him that fateful day were gone. Powerful men had tried to silence him once. They wouldn't hesitate to do it again. It was up to him to expose the truth.

Too bad he had no idea whom he could trust.

When he finished with the fire, he stood. "I'll make coffee."

Hawk went into the kitchen and opened the cabinet that housed the coffee maker. He filled the carafe with water and added scoops of coffee from the can he kept in the freezer. As the coffee dripped, he did a quick mental inventory of his house back in Brookland. He had no doubt that at some point the professional hit men would go back to the scene of their failure, eventually identifying him as the one who'd helped Jillian and Lizzy escape.

They wouldn't find anything personal at his place. He didn't have a home office, preferring, instead, to work in the small space he rented in the strip mall not far from where he lived. The only information he kept at his office was related to his clients. All of his personal paperwork, most of which had been expertly forged two years ago, was kept in a safe deposit box at the bank.

For years, he'd thought his secret was safe. Until now. How long before the hit men put two and two together to figure out that Hawk Jacobson was really James Wade?

Based on the extensive governmental resources he believed Barton had at his disposal? Not long.

Feeling grim, he realized they'd be forced to move locations first thing in the morning. And go where? He had no clue.

"I can't drink coffee this late," Jillian said. He glanced over to find her standing on the other side of the room, her arms crossed over her chest as if she didn't dare get too close. "But I think we need to call the police. Now. Tonight."

He didn't answer, mostly because he wasn't sure what to say. He wanted, needed to tell her the truth, but this didn't seem like the proper time or place.

She wouldn't appreciate his view that going to the authorities could very well be like stepping on a rotten log, allowing professional hit men to pour out like termites.

"Calling the police is what normal people do," Jillian insisted. "Just because you happen to be a private investigator, it doesn't mean we shouldn't let the authorities know that two men came into my house with weapons with the intent to kill me."

"Actually, we don't really know what they intended to do."

She scowled. "I'm pretty sure they didn't intend to play nice with their guns."

It was a good point. He decided to probe further. "Does the name Senator Barton mean anything to you?"

She blinked in confusion. "Senator Rick Barton? Not really. I mean, I know he sits on a committee related to the Department of Defense, but I can't even tell you what state he's from or what he looks like."

"He sits on the Armed Services Committee," Hawk corrected. "He's a senator from Virginia and happens to be good friends with Todd Hayes, the current Secretary of Defense." He waited for some sort of recognition to dawn in her eyes, but she only shrugged.

"Yeah, okay. That sounds right. I'm not totally up on all the players in our government, but whatever. I don't see what either of those guys has to do with your decision to postpone calling the police."

"Powerful people in high places can convince the cops to turn a blind eye to what might be happening under their nose." He hesitated, the holes in his memory making it difficult to say anything with certainty. All he remembered was seeing Major Rick Barton deep in the hills where he wasn't supposed to be. He sensed there was more but couldn't bring the fragments of his memory together into a full picture.

Now she looked annoyed. "Oh, come on—" She abruptly cut off what she was about to say when Lizzy began to cry.

"Mommy! Mommy! Bad mans are coming to get me!"

Jillian spun on her heel and charged into the bedroom. Hawk stayed where he was, unwilling to add to Lizzy's frightened state. He knew she'd watched him holding a gun on one of the intruders and was reliving that scary moment in her nightmares.

He poured himself a cup of coffee and sat down at the kitchen table. He needed to think. To understand what was going on so he could plan his next steps. A good soldier always had at least one backup plan.

Several things bothered him. Why had Barton decided to send hit men after Jillian tonight? The fact that James Wade had married her five years ago wasn't a secret. The army knew about Jillian, they'd provided her benefits while he was overseas, and he assumed they'd provided death benefits after he'd been pronounced dead, despite how they'd obviously never found his body.

So why now?

And why not wait until the dead of night rather than 10:30 p.m.? The two guys had been professionals, but they were clearly not prepared to face an opponent like Hawk—someone with equal or better training than they had. Whoever provided the intel must have mentioned they were facing a grade school teacher and a four-year-old child. Not a soldier.

The burn of anger at the thought of those two men getting their hands on Jillian and Lizzy was difficult to ignore. But anger, much like indecision, was the enemy.

He took a deep breath and let it out, slowly. He toyed with the idea of calling Mike Callahan, a former private investigator he'd once worked with. Mike had recently gotten married and had taken a position with the sheriff's department. Mike owed him a favor, and Hawk could easily collect. Not that he'd really have to use the favor as leverage. Hawk knew that Mike, or any of the Callahan siblings, would help him out, no questions asked. That was the type of family they were. The Callahans had welcomed him into their home and made him feel like he was one of them.

Still, he preferred to work alone. At least for now. But he wouldn't risk any harm coming to Jillian or Lizzy.

What he really wanted to do was to stash Jillian and Lizzy someplace safe while he continued working the case. Should he send her to stay with the Callahans? They were about the only people he trusted. Yet at the same time, he didn't dare let Jillian and Lizzy out of his sight.

Not when he knew that he was the only reason they were in danger.

He scrubbed his hands over his face, fighting a wave of exhaustion. Jillian deserved to know the truth about his real identity. Yet he worried how she'd react. Five months ago, when he'd found her, he had moved in next door as a way to help her out. He'd noticed the plain gold wedding ring on her finger without the diamond engagement ring he'd given her. That, along with her little girl, had convinced him she'd moved on with another man. He couldn't blame her since he was legally dead.

But he'd been wrong.

He had a daughter. The news was stunning and he realized he should have figured it out sooner. He wanted to talk to Jillian but feared she'd be upset with him when she learned the truth. And worst of all, she might feel as if she needed to stay with him to honor their five-year-old wedding vows despite the horrible scars that grooved his face.

She was the beauty and he was the beast. With a face that scared Lizzy. He hated knowing his own daughter was frightened of him. Yet he couldn't change who he was. Who he'd become.

When it was clear Jillian wasn't returning to the kitchen to pick up the conversation where they'd left it off, he dumped the dregs of his coffee in the sink and made his way into his room.

Tomorrow morning, he'd have several decisions to make. They'd need a new place to go and they needed to air the truth.

If she was angry with him, then fine. He'd take her anger over her pity any day of the week.

Jillian fell asleep comforting Lizzy, only to wake up at dawn with a crick in her neck.

Stretching with a muffled groan, she eased out from Lizzy's bed. She tiptoed out of the room to use the bathroom and then headed into the kitchen, shivering a bit in the cool air.

There was no sign of Hawk. Clearly, he hadn't followed through on her request to call the police.

Even now his reluctance made no sense. But enough was enough. Better late than never, right? She went over to her purse and dug out her cell phone.

One bar, indicating the battery was nearly dead. Great. She didn't have a charger and, from what she could tell, there wasn't one around here, either. The place was comfortable but rustic.

She stared at the screen, wondering who would respond if she called 911. Surely not anyone from the Brookland Police Department, which was where the crime had taken place.

"What are you doing?"

Hawk's hoarse voice was so unexpected she let out a yelp and almost dropped the phone.

"You shouldn't sneak up on me like that." She knew

she sounded cranky, but seriously, the man needed to wear a cowbell around his neck.

"Don't call the police yet. Not until we talk."

Now he was reading her mind? Ugh. She turned the phone off to preserve what was left of her battery and tucked it into the pocket of her sweatshirt. "Talking isn't exactly your strength," she felt compelled to point out.

The right corner of his mouth kicked up in what may have been the hint of a smile. The first she'd ever seen from him. "Maybe not, but you'll want to hear my story."

His story? The one behind his scar? He was right about that, since she'd been wondering about his story for the past five months.

"Sounds like we'll need coffee." She moved into the kitchen and made a fresh pot of coffee. While she did that Hawk opened a cupboard and pulled out a box of instant oatmeal packets.

"This is about all I have on hand for breakfast," he said, his voice full of apology. "Or we can stop for breakfast when we leave."

"Leave?" Once again he knocked her off-balance. "Why are we leaving so soon?"

He didn't answer right away, a trait that annoyed her.

"Well?" She pulled two mugs out of the cabinet and set them beside the coffeepot. "I thought you said we were safe here."

He filled a teapot with water and put it on the stove. "We are, but it's only a matter of time before they track us here."

Her stomach clenched. "They? Who?"

"The men who came for you last night. They'll find out my name and will search for my license plate number and for any other properties that I might own. That will lead them here, to this cabin."

His words sent a chill down her spine. "Okay, now you're scaring me."

"I know. I'm sorry, but we'll stay one step ahead of them."

She poured two mugs of coffee and, since there wasn't any milk, made do with adding sugar to hers before handing him the one that was black. Their fingers brushed and she was startled by the tingle of awareness she felt. What was wrong with her? This was the wrong time, wrong place and definitely the wrong man!

"You said we need to talk."

He nodded before taking a sip from his mug. "It's a long story, goes back a couple of years."

"Okay." She took a seat at the table. "I'm listening."

"I used to be in the military," he said, his blue gaze centered on hers.

"I thought so," she said with a nod. "Just like James." At his silent stare, she added, "My husband."

"Yeah. Well." Hawk looked away, clearly uncomfortable. "I—I did a lot of work that was considered classified."

Just like James, but this time she didn't voice the comparison out loud.

"I was on a team with three other guys," he went on and suddenly a bad feeling came over her.

"You were with James, weren't you? Is that what you've been trying to tell me? That you knew my husband?" She knew her voice was getting louder but couldn't stop it. "All this time, you knew James but never said anything?"

"Jilly, please, just listen for a minute," he begged.

She sucked in a harsh breath. "What did you call me?"

Hawk winced and blanched. "I—uh, I'm sorry. I didn't mean to be so familiar…"

"No." She rose to her feet and took a step back from him, her mind whirling. He'd called her Jilly, just like James used to.

Then she remembered that brief moment in the bedroom when she'd thought Hawk was actually James. She stared at him, her thoughts spinning out of control.

"Jillian, I'm sorry to tell you like this. But I was sent on a secret mission, and me and my team saw something we shouldn't have. We were flown home to be debriefed by the Pentagon, only there was a storm that took us further west. We ended up landing in Columbus, Ohio, and they stuck us in a small prop plane. We crashed in the Appalachian Mountains. Everyone died in the crash except for me. And I—" his voice trailed off for a long moment before he continued "—I was badly injured. I had no memory, no ability to walk, my face was damaged beyond recognition and I still don't know how I managed to survive."

"You—you're James?" The blood drained from her face and she collapsed in the chair she'd just vacated. "I don't understand."

"I'm Hawk," he corrected. "I didn't even remember my name for a full year. I only remember watching hawks flying over my head for days on end, so that's the name I went with. I picked Jacobson because I had some dim memory of my father being named Jacob."

Her heart squeezed in her chest at what he'd gone through. Then she realized what he'd said. "But you did eventually realize you were James, right? And chose not to come home to me. To us."

"That's not entirely true. I didn't remember you right away, and when I did, there were only bits and pieces. I stayed away because after the crash I saw men combing the woods, searching for me." Hawk's expression went cold. "They were not there to rescue me but to kill me. They had guns, Jilly. And if the older couple who'd found me hadn't sheltered me from those men, I wouldn't be here now."

"But what about five months ago?" she persisted. "You moved in next door to me on purpose, didn't you?"

"Yes." The teakettle whistled and he quickly removed it from the burner. "I came to Milwaukee because I knew you had family here and wouldn't have stayed at Fort Bragg. Even then, it took me a while to find you in Brookland. Once I did, I couldn't stay away. I needed to make sure you were safe."

She couldn't argue that he had saved them.

"I want you to know I won't hold you to anything," Hawk continued. "James as you knew him is gone. Hawk was the lone survivor of that plane crash. Where we go from here is totally up to you."

"Where we go from here?" The realization of what he was saying sank deep.

Hawk was James. He was her *husband*. Lizzy's *father*.

And she had absolutely no idea where to go from here.

THREE

Hawk busied himself with making a bowl of instant oatmeal for Jillian. The truth hung between them like a dark storm cloud, threatening to burst, bringing snow and ice pelting down. Telling her the story wasn't as difficult as he'd anticipated, but he wasn't sure the truth had fully sunk in yet.

He'd been honest with her when he'd claimed James was dead. That year he spent hiding in the mountains, recuperating from his injuries, had changed him. James had died in the plane crash, leaving a man called Hawk behind.

That he'd survived when the rest of his team had died haunted him still. The Callahans would claim God had a plan, but he didn't believe it. Not the way he used to. He'd lost his entire life that day.

Even now, sometimes he awoke from a nightmare, hearing his team's screams as the plane plummeted down into the mountainside. Only to realize it was his throat that was sore from screaming.

His time on the mountain was a blur. He'd lost track of the days that had passed, the hours that had gone by while he watched a pair of hawks flying high in the sky.

He'd dragged himself down the mountain, inch by painful inch, with no particular destination in mind. Thankfully, he'd eventually come across a cabin tucked into the woods. It was actually the garden offering fresh vegetables that had caught his eye. He'd been helping himself to fresh tomatoes and cucumbers when Jolene and Ken Thornhill had found him.

Ken had carried a shotgun, but one look at Hawk's scars had him putting the weapon away. Hawk had convinced them not to call the authorities, and the couple, being mountain people and distrustful of the cops anyway, had readily agreed. The Thornhills helped get him back on his feet. Their home remedies worked just as well as any hospital-based therapy.

Except for the scar.

And when the men with guns had come looking for him, they'd hidden him in their root cellar until they were gone. Hawk was convinced the men were soldiers sent by Barton to find him and silence him for good. Especially since the plane had gone down after conveniently springing a fuel leak.

He owed the Thornhills his life. But they hadn't wanted any form of payment. He'd sent them cash when he'd managed to work enough to get some, but the money had come back to him as undeliverable.

Shaking himself from thoughts of the past, he carried the bowl of oatmeal to the table and set it in front of Jillian. She hadn't said anything for the past several minutes and, even now, avoided looking directly at him.

"Eat," he encouraged softly. "You'll need to keep up your strength."

She obediently picked up the spoon and took a small bite. Lizzy chose that moment to come out of the bedroom rubbing her sleepy eyes, looking adorable in her pink footie pajamas.

"I hav'ta go potty."

"Sure. This way, sweetie." Jillian jumped up from the table and crossed over to their daughter, steering her into the bathroom.

Hawk put the kettle back on to boil, hoping Lizzy liked oatmeal. He had no idea what his daughter liked to eat or her favorite things to do. He'd noticed a dollhouse in the corner of her bedroom and now wished he'd thought to bring some of the dolls along for her to play with.

At least she had her teddy bear. The one she'd clutched protectively as he'd pulled her from beneath the bed.

He glanced at his watch, estimating how much time they had before they needed to hit the road. Less than an hour. Doable, but only if Jillian and Lizzy finished their breakfast ASAP.

The teakettle whistled as Jillian and Lizzy emerged from the bathroom. Lizzy clapped her hands over her ears.

"Too loud!"

Hawk winced, nodded and moved the kettle, adding hot water to two more bowls of oatmeal. Then he carried them to the kitchen table, setting one down near Jillian's bowl and taking his to the other side.

Jillian lifted Lizzy onto her lap. It pained him to know Lizzy wouldn't want to sit with him. As he watched, Jillian bowed her head and softly thanked God for the food she was about to eat. He was reminded of how the Callahans always prayed out loud before meals, but he'd never joined in.

No one spoke for several long moments as they ate. And it was Lizzy who eventually broke the silence.

"Can we go home, Mommy?"

The question hit him in the face like a blow. He looked at Jillian, unsure if he should speak up or not.

"Not today, sweetie." Jillian hitched the little girl higher on her lap. "Finish up your oatmeal like a good girl."

"We can try to find a place that's kid-friendly," he offered. "I know a place that rents individual cabins. It's not too far away and has a playground I'm sure Lizzy would love."

Jillian shrugged. "Whatever you think is best. We'll make the most of wherever we end up, won't we Lizzy-girl?"

Lizzy nodded her head, her drooping pigtails bobbing up and down. His daughter's hair was dark, like his, without any sign of Jillian's reddish glints. But the rest of her features were mirror images of her mother's. She'd be just as beautiful as Jillian someday.

He finished his meal before they did and carried his dishes to the sink. "We'll need to leave soon."

"Okay." Jillian's voice sounded resigned.

There was no point in saying anything further; moving again was necessary in order to keep them alive. And while he still felt terrible knowing that he'd brought danger to their doorstep, the only thing he could do now was to stay ahead of the danger curve.

He took his turn in the bathroom, spending less than ten minutes. He heard Jillian and Lizzy's voices in their bedroom and hoped they were getting their things together.

Thankfully, Jillian had done the dishes, so there was

nothing more that needed his attention. He pulled on his leather coat, grabbed his keys and waited, gazing out through the large picture window of the living room.

A movement outside caught his attention. He froze, his gaze tracking the shifting of leaves and the sudden uprising of a bird from the bushes.

Too late! They'd found the cabin.

He hurried into the bedroom as Jillian was trying to coax the teddy bear from Lizzy's grip. "We need to go. Get your coats, leave the duffel behind. We're heading out the back."

"The back?" The confusion in Jillian's green gaze morphed into fear. She instantly yanked the bear away, shoved Lizzy's coat on, then hers, before lifting Lizzy into her arms. She returned the teddy bear hoping the stuffed animal would help keep Lizzy calm. Her voice dropped to a whisper. "They're here?"

He nodded, gently pulling her toward him. Ushering her into his bedroom and to the back doorway he had built in there just for this type of thing, he considered their options. First, they needed to get out of the cabin and deeper into the woods without leaving a blatant footprint trail behind. Using the SUV was out of the question; the hostiles were too close. He'd have to make do with the snowmobile he had hidden in the woods toward the back of his property.

Outside, the December air was crisp and cool despite the sunshine. Keeping Jillian in front of him, he covered their backs as he guided them into the woods. He could tell Jillian was trying to move silently, but to his ears it sounded as if they were a stampede of elephants announcing their location to anyone within a fifty-mile radius. He worried, too, about leaving footprints in the snow. The snow wasn't deep and there were spots where there were leafy areas to step on as a way to mitigate the risk.

Thankfully, Lizzy didn't say anything but kept her head tucked against her mother's shoulder, still gripping the tattered teddy bear. He wished the little girl trusted him enough to allow him to carry her, knowing they'd be able to move more quickly. But he didn't want to risk her tears.

Knowing the woods helped. Prior to renting the house next to Jillian's he'd spent a lot of time up here. The place had reminded him of the Thornhill cabin in the mountains.

The cluster of bushes he'd been aiming for was straight ahead. He picked up his pace, moving ahead. Jillian did her best to keep up, but her foot got caught on a branch. He managed to catch her before she hit the ground.

He gently set her on her feet and gestured toward the cluster of bushes. She nodded her understanding and headed in that direction. Hawk continued sweeping his gaze over the area, looking for signs the hostiles were near, surprised that they hadn't covered the back side of the cabin but had chosen to come in from the front and the west.

Although he knew there very well could be more.

When they reached the cluster of bushes, he carved out a small space with his hands and drew Jillian down. "Stay here, I'll be back soon."

She clutched at his arm. "Don't leave us," she begged.

It wasn't by choice but out of necessity. He leaned down so his mouth was near her ear. "I have a snowmobile nearby. I promise I'll be quick."

Tears welled in her eyes, but she gave a jerky nod, showing she understood. He drew out his gun and handed it to her. This time she didn't protest but clutched it with both hands while keeping one arm around Lizzy, holding her close.

He hesitated. There was so much he wanted to say, but there wasn't time. He needed to move, to draw the hostiles away from Jillian and Lizzy.

He'd willingly sacrifice himself to keep them alive and safe.

This was so much worse than waiting in the car. Since they were surrounded by snow-covered trees and bushes, any sense of being safe was eroded by the cold breeze that made her shiver. Her fingers were beginning to go numb, but she didn't dare let go of the gun.

She silently prayed that God would watch over them. Keeping an internal monologue in her head helped keep her fear in check. Hawk would return for them. He had a snowmobile nearby and would be here soon. He wouldn't let the men combing the woods reach her and Lizzy.

Hawk was James, except he wasn't. Her husband had never moved so stealthily. Her husband had smiled and laughed often, and while he may not have been verbose, he certainly had spoken more than Hawk did.

Nevertheless, he was her husband. She was still married to the man. Wasn't she? Maybe not, since James had been declared dead. But he wasn't dead, not really. He was just—different. Thinking about it made her head hurt. It was all so confusing.

Come on, Hawk, where are you?

"Mommy?" Lizzy lifted her head.

"Shh," she whispered.

Lizzy wiggled a little and Jillian feared her daughter wasn't going to stay silent much longer. Hoping and praying Hawk would return soon, she kept her mouth right near her daughter's ear.

"Be quiet for just a little while longer."

Lizzy nodded her head and leaned against her, rubbing her cheek against the teddy bear's head.

Jillian let out a sigh of relief. So far, so good.

A twig snapped. The sound sent a stab of terror deep into her stomach. She went still, her breath locked in her throat and her heart thundering in her chest. She pressed Lizzy's face against her chest, hoping the little girl wouldn't do or say something to give them away.

Since rediscovering the church after moving to Wisconsin, she'd leaned on God often and didn't hesitate to do that again, now.

Please keep us safe, Lord! Please!

The sound of rustling leaves seemed close. She imagined one of the black ski-masked men making his way toward their hiding spot. How much longer? She dreaded every passing second, fearing the worst.

Then abruptly there was an *oomph* sound and a muffled thud. Still, she didn't move, didn't so much as blink. She wanted desperately to believe Hawk had taken care of the guy, but for all she knew, he'd fallen flat on his face the way she nearly had a few minutes ago.

Another ten seconds passed. She strained to listen but heard nothing.

Suddenly Hawk loomed in front of them, a streak of dirt covering his scar. He gave a nod and held out his hand. She shakily put her hand in his, allowing him to pull her and Lizzy to her feet.

She wanted to ask what was going on, but as if he

sensed her intent, he lifted a finger to his lips. She nodded in understanding.

They weren't safe yet. And it struck her then that they may never be safe again.

From this moment on, safety could very well be nothing more than an illusion.

Hawk gently but firmly pulled her in a different direction. She couldn't tell if they were going closer toward the cabin or farther away. It wasn't easy to navigate while carrying Lizzy, because she couldn't see her feet. Twice she felt a branch of some sort pressing against her shin, making her lift her foot higher to get over it.

They moved through the dense woods in what felt like slow motion. But soon enough, Hawk tugged on her arm, indicating they could stop here.

She glanced around, thinking she'd find the snowmobile he'd mentioned. When she didn't see it, her hopes plummeted. Had someone stolen it? Or had the ski-mask guys found it before Hawk had?

Hawk stepped over to a bush and began moving snow-laden branches. Her eyes widened in surprise when she saw the camouflage-green snowmobile hidden behind the shrubbery.

It took Hawk a while to get the thing uncovered. It soon became clear that the bush hadn't been a bush at all but dozens of loose branches placed strategically around the machine.

He swung his leg over the seat and gestured for her to get on in front of him. She hesitated, worried about Lizzy.

"Keep her in front of you," he whispered.

She nodded and did as he asked. The seat seemed far

too small for the three of them but her protest was swallowed by the roar of the engine.

She felt Lizzy shuddering against her, guessing that the little girl hated the loud sound. Hawk hit the gas and the machine moved forward, the twin skis gliding over the snow, fallen branches and leaves. She let out a screech as he went even faster, tearing a path through the woods.

Stealth was not an option now. The way they roared through the woods broadcasted their location to anyone still searching for them. Clutching Hawk's knee with one arm, while clinging to Lizzy with the other, she grew convinced that he was the only one capable of getting them out of there.

But where would they go? It wasn't as if you could drive a snowmobile down the center of a plowed road. Or could you? Maybe. Yet as fast as they were moving, she knew the machine carrying them didn't have the necessary speed to outrun a car.

Bare branches slapped her in the face, making her eyes sting with tears. She curled her body around Lizzy's, protecting the little girl the only way she could.

The trees thinned and she wondered if they were getting close to the road or to the end of Hawk's property. She felt certain they'd escaped, until she heard the loud echo of gunfire above the drone of the engine.

No! Jillian gasped, horrified that the ski-masked men were still out there, shooting at them.

"Keep your head down," he ordered.

Doing anything else was impossible anyway, but what about Hawk? He was the most exposed, and if something happened to him…there was no hope for her and Lizzy to survive.

She prayed again as Hawk continued driving. The woods seemed to go on forever, thinning out a bit, then growing thicker again. She had no idea how much land Hawk owned, or if they were out on someone else's property by now.

Did it matter if they were? It gave her a measure of hope that the owners might call the police.

The gunfire had stopped, but she couldn't relax. Not with Hawk still driving like a maniac.

Then he abruptly pulled over and stopped the machine. Silence reigned except for the ringing in her ears.

"Take Lizzy and stand over there for a minute," Hawk said, urging her off the snowmobile and pointing at a pine tree.

She wanted to protest but knew it was useless. She awkwardly climbed off the machine, feeling Lizzy's weight slipping down.

Hawk jumped back on the snowmobile and rode it about eighty yards away before abandoning it. Then he pulled several items out of a storage area behind the seat, before hurrying toward her. He was careful to step only on the tracks made by the sled.

She was impressed by his actions, knowing the machine would draw the men in the woods away from them. She hitched Lizzy in her arms.

"I'll take her." Hawk didn't wait for permission but took Lizzy from her, after storing what looked like duct tape and twine in his jacket pocket. "This way."

Lizzy didn't cry, too frightened to do anything but hang on. They once again moved through the woods, faster now that Jillian wasn't impeded by her daughter's weight.

Hawk stopped in front of a large tree. "We're going up."

Her jaw dropped. "Up? The tree?"

He nodded, pulling another length of twine out of his jacket pocket. "I'll carry you while you hold Lizzy."

She shook her head, thinking he was crazy. No way could Hawk carry both of them all the way up a tree. And what would they do when they got up there? Swing from the branches like Tarzan and Jane? She'd fall on her face for sure.

"Like this." He placed Lizzy back in her arms. "You're going to put your arms around my neck and lock your legs around my waist, keeping Lizzy tucked between us."

"She'll fall," she protested.

"She won't. She'll hang on to you. Trust me."

She did trust Hawk. Had trusted him to get them out of danger twice now. Knew that God was somehow guiding him.

"Hold tight, Lizzy." The little girl nodded and wrapped her tiny arms snugly around her neck. Then Jillian faced Hawk's back and locked her arms around his chest. When she lifted her legs around his waist, pressing Lizzy securely between them, he began to climb, using the rope around the tree for leverage.

How he made it up the tree was a mystery. The muscles of his chest and shoulders bunched beneath her arms with the strain, but he didn't make a sound as he went vertical.

She wasn't sure what she expected, but the flat platform about two-thirds of the way up the tree was a surprise. Especially when she saw that there were three full sides to the thing that protected them from view. Hawk managed to get up and over the edge of the platform, landing on his hands and knees.

"You can get off now," he whispered.

It was scary being up so high, but she unlocked her

legs first, then slid to the side so she was sitting on the platform next to him. Holding Lizzy close, she edged closer to the trunk of the tree, seeking some sense of stability.

"We made it," she whispered in awe.

Hawk nodded. "We still need to be quiet, okay?" He didn't wait for a response but pulled out his gun and flattened himself against the platform. He inched to the edge, peering down to see what was going on down below.

She lifted her hand to push her hair out of her face, frowning when she saw blood. For a moment she didn't understand, but then she noticed several more drops of blood staining the platform.

He'd been shot!

FOUR

"Hawk! You're hurt!" Jillian whispered in a low, urgent tone.

"It's nothing. Keep Lizzy quiet, okay?" Ignoring the pain in his shoulder, Hawk looked carefully over the edge of the deer blind, searching for hostiles. He had two guns and a knife but didn't want to use them unless there was absolutely no other option. He'd taken one man temporarily out of commission, but there were three more, and he couldn't bear the thought of Jillian and Lizzy witnessing him killing a man.

Yet he'd do whatever was necessary to keep them safe.

They were in danger because of him. Because he'd poked the sleeping bear by probing for information on Senator Barton. It was the only thing that made sense.

Pushing the thought away, he kept his gaze focused on the wooded area below while internally planning their next move. He needed to call Mike Callahan for help, but he wasn't thrilled with the idea of putting his buddy in danger.

Jillian did her best to soothe Lizzy, urging the little girl to stay quiet. Lizzy's hiccuping sobs were muffled against Jillian's chest and he hated knowing his daughter was so frightened.

Peering through the trees, he could see the dark shape of the snowmobile where he'd left it, eighty yards from where they were hiding.

Time to implement the next phase of his plan.

"Stay up here with Lizzy," he whispered to Jillian.

"Where are you going?" There was thinly veiled panic in her voice.

He wasn't sure how to answer her without causing her to become even more afraid. He trusted his ability to take out the three men but hated leaving her here, alone. Pulling out his phone, he found Mike Callahan's number and showed it to her. "If I'm not back in an hour, call Mike. He's a cop and will keep you and Lizzy safe."

"Why can't we call him now?" Jillian argued. "Then you can stay here with us."

"He's at least forty-five minutes away, maybe more." He thrust the phone at her. "Please, Jilly. I'm asking you to trust me on this."

She held his gaze for a long moment, before reluctantly nodding. He wanted nothing more than to pull her close in a reassuring hug but needed to get moving.

Soundlessly, he climbed down the tree, ignoring his injured shoulder, and moved quickly without the added burden of having to carry Jillian and Lizzy. On the ground, he took a moment to get his bearings.

He found a branch and used it to help wipe away his footprints from the base of the tree. Then he took a roundabout and silent path toward the snowmobile.

Hawk halted behind a tree when he caught sight of one hostile positioned twenty yards in front of him. Hawk could only see his back, it was clear the man's attention was focused on the snowmobile.

His mistake. Hawk managed to sneak up on him from

behind, taking him down without making much of a sound despite the ache in his shoulder. Hawk knocked him unconscious, then bound and gagged him using the duct tape in his pocket.

Another one down, two more to go.

Hawk moved silently away, estimating that another assailant would be at the three o'clock position. Hiding behind a tree, he searched for a sign and then found him.

The second guy didn't go down as quietly as the first one. Could be because Hawk was feeling the effect of blood loss, but he refused to acknowledge weakness. When he had the second man unconscious and tied up securely, as well, he looked for the next one.

Keenly aware of the minutes ticking by on his allotted hour, he hoped Jillian wouldn't place the call to Mike before he'd had the chance to take the last attacker out of commission.

Hawk knew that taking down the last man would be the most difficult. The hostile must know that his cohorts were compromised and would have no reason to stay at his point location.

Ducking behind a thorny bush, Hawk wiped snow away to uncover a large rock. He tossed it high in the air, then crouched down and watched carefully for signs of movement when it landed with a dull thud.

For several long seconds there was nothing, but finally, the slightest movement from the twelve o'clock position caught his eye. Target in sight, Hawk moved in.

Another movement had him dropping to the ground. The sound of gunfire echoed loudly through the woods, narrowly missing him. Gut instinct had Hawk rolling to the side and returning fire at the spot where he'd seen the muzzle flash.

Then there was nothing but silence.

Because he'd hit his target? He wasn't sure.

He waited another five minutes before edging along the ground toward the nine o'clock position. The man was lying there, dead from a gunshot wound to his chest.

Hawk sighed and rose to his feet, staggering a bit. Four men taken down total, one dead. A wave of despair hit him hard. He hated knowing that he'd killed a man even though it was in self-defense.

After a long moment, he pulled off the man's ski mask, realizing this guy was the same one who'd been in Jillian's house. Searching for ID proved fruitless, but he did find a set of car keys. Hawk tucked them away. Returning to the snowmobile, he fired it up and rode back to the tree with the deer blind.

"Jillian? You and Lizzy okay?"

"Yes," came the faint response. "Just cold."

"I know. Did you call Mike?"

"Not yet."

"Good." He gathered every ounce of strength and determination, knowing he'd need it get up the tree and back down with Lizzy and Jillian. It was much harder this time: his left arm was weak and he didn't have the same surge of adrenaline roaring through his veins. But he managed, and soon the three of them were back on solid ground.

"Now what?" Jillian asked, her body shivering with cold.

He indicated the snowmobile. "Now we find the vehicle belonging to the men who came to find us."

She looked as if she wanted to argue, but he gestured for her to get on the snowmobile first with Lizzy. He slid in behind them and reached out to grab the handlebars.

The trip to the highway didn't take long, and he quickly found the black SUV, a newer make and model compared to his own.

"We need Lizzy's car seat," Jillian protested as he ushered them inside.

"I know." Hawk didn't want to stay at the cabin for much longer, fearing more men were on the way, but the cabin was only a half mile up the road. Getting the car seat didn't take much time, and soon they were back on the highway.

He cranked the heat for Jillian and Lizzy while considering their next move. They'd been found at the cabin far too quickly. He never should have gone there in the first place.

The weight of Jillian's and Lizzy's safety was incredibly heavy on his shoulders.

He couldn't afford to make another mistake.

Jillian gratefully absorbed the warm air blasting from the vents of the SUV. She'd prayed the entire time they'd been up in the tree stand, and God had answered by not only keeping them safe but providing a method of escape.

Between Hawk's ingenuity and God's support, they'd made it out the woods alive. Yet it was difficult to relax. She felt certain the danger was far from over.

She wrestled with the fact that Hawk was really James. She'd lived next door to him for five months—how could she not have figured it out? This all seemed like some sort of twisted movie plot rather than something that happened in real life.

She glanced over at him, searching his profile for signs of the man she'd once married.

Now that she knew the truth, it was easy to spot the

similarities and differences. His intense blue eyes were the same, but the prominent cheekbones were gone, and she felt bad about the deep scar grooving his face. Hawk was leaner and more muscular than she remembered, and his voice, which always sounded hoarse now, made her wonder if there had been some sort of internal damage to his vocal cords as a result of the plane crash.

Hawk didn't laugh the way James had, or talk as much. He was serious and to the point.

She turned away, mourning the loss all over again. Maybe Hawk was right to claim James had died in the Appalachian Mountains. The man sitting beside her, the one who'd climbed up and down a tree with her and Lizzy on his back, seemed very different than the man she'd married.

And for the life of her, she couldn't look at him and think *James*. He was Hawk.

"You'll need to stop at a drugstore. I need bandages and other supplies to take care of your wound."

He gave a small nod. "Later. Right now I need to figure out a place to go where we'll be safe."

"You mentioned a place with individual cabins and a playground for Lizzy," she reminded.

He hesitated and shrugged. "Yeah, that's where we're headed. But it's just five days before Christmas and I'm not sure they have openings."

"I can't imagine individual cabins being a hot place to spend Christmas."

He glanced at her in surprise. "It is for me."

"Because you're a single guy without a family." The minute the words were out of her mouth, she wished them back. "I mean, until now."

Hawk didn't respond and she knew that she'd stuck

her foot in her mouth, big-time. Yet it was hardly her fault. She'd only known he was James for a few hours.

Terrifying hours that they'd spent hiding from armed men wearing ski masks.

The silence grew uncomfortable. More proof that they were virtual strangers rather than husband and wife.

"How do you know about this place with cabins and a playground anyway?"

"Used it last summer when a friend of mine needed to hide out for a while."

"Mike Callahan? That friend?"

He nodded.

More silence, and it occurred to her that attempting to have a conversation with Hawk was harder work than panning for gold. Not that she'd ever tried panning for gold.

"I'm sorry," she finally said.

He frowned. "For what?"

She let out a sigh. "For insinuating that you don't have a family. It's just—difficult to wrap my mind around all of this."

"Understandable. And as I said before, it doesn't have to change anything between us."

But it did, she thought. Knowing Hawk was James changed *everything.*

She found herself thinking about the future more than ever. How her relationship with Hawk would move forward after the danger was over.

"Mommy, I'm hungry," Lizzy said plaintively.

Glancing at the clock, she was surprised to see it was approaching eleven o'clock in the morning. Considering they'd been up by six and running for their lives since seven, she couldn't blame Lizzy for wanting to eat.

"We'll stop at a restaurant soon," Hawk surprised her by saying. "There's one not too far away. And there's a drugstore nearby, too."

She was glad to hear they'd soon have the supplies they needed to tend to his wound.

"Can I have chicken strips?" Lizzy asked.

Jillian smiled. "Sure."

"Okay." Lizzy was satisfied with that response.

"I take it those are her favorites?" Hawk asked.

"Yes. With lots of ketchup." She was saddened by the fact that Hawk didn't know these small details about his daughter. Her favorite foods, favorite books, her friends at day care.

Five months that they could have spent getting re-united had been wasted. In fact, she doubted that Hawk would have come clean at all if it hadn't been for her need to be rescued.

"You have no idea who they were?" She glanced over her shoulder at Lizzy to make sure she wasn't listen-ing. Amazingly, despite running for their lives, riding a snowmobile and going up into a tree, Lizzy still had her ragged teddy bear. Her cheek was resting on the teddy bear's head, her eyes drooping with sleepiness.

"No. Other than I assume they were sent by either Barton or Hayes."

"But why come to my house?" Jillian asked.

Hawk glanced at her. "It's no secret we were once married. The only thing I can figure out is that they in-tended to kidnap you and Lizzy in order to get me to come out of hiding."

Chills rippled down her spine at his theory. "But that doesn't make any sense. It wouldn't have worked. I didn't even know you were alive until this morning."

"They didn't know that," Hawk reasoned. "I have to assume that my prying into Senator Barton's past triggered several alarms. They'd never found my body after the plane crash but probably chalked that up to me crawling off somewhere to die."

"Maybe." She wasn't convinced.

"It's possible they now believe we've been in touch with each other over the years."

Ridiculous, since there had been no contact since the day she'd been informed that James had died.

"That was the worst day of my life," she said in a low voice.

"What was?"

She struggled to ward off tears. "Finding out you were dead on the same day I discovered I was pregnant."

Hawk's grip on the steering wheel tightened to the point his knuckles went white. A thick, heavy silence hung between them for several miles. "I'm sorry you had to go through that," he finally managed.

She sniffled and swiped at her face. Why she was getting all emotional over this, she had no idea. She felt guilty for making him feel bad. "It was hardly your fault. It was just—rotten timing."

"Yeah." There was a pause, then he asked, "Who came to see you?"

She shook her head helplessly. "I can't remember his name now but probably have it at home somewhere. I think he left his card. Master Sergeant Somebody-or-other."

"I'm surprised you kept it all these years."

"I kept a lot of things over the years." There was no reason to feel defensive, and she tried to tone it down.

"I have several pictures of us together. I show them to Lizzy so she'll remember you."

"That's, uh, nice." Hawk's tone held uncertainty and she realized she'd done it again. Lizzy didn't have to remember her father from a photo.

He was here now. He looked different, yes, but he was still her father. And they needed to find a time to tell the little girl that Hawk was her daddy.

Which also meant that in the eyes of God, they were still married.

All at once, it all seemed overwhelming. She'd made a life for herself and Lizzy, and now things would never be the same. Hawk deserved to spend time with his daughter, she wouldn't keep that from him.

And what about the two of them? What had he said earlier? That he wouldn't hold her to anything? What did that even mean? She'd loved James with her whole heart.

But there was no denying Hawk was mostly a stranger.

She'd never been with another man, not even on a date. At first it had been because of Lizzy. Being a single mother, even with her mother's support, had been difficult.

Four months after Lizzy's first birthday, her mother had suffered a stroke and died. Leaving Jillian and Lizzy alone, again.

"I'm sorry," Hawk said, reaching over to put his hand on her knee. "I'm sure it was difficult raising Lizzy by yourself."

She stared at his broad, calloused hand, wishing she dared take it in hers. She hated this awkwardness between them. "I have a box of your things saved in the basement, too." She hoped changing the subject might ease the tension. "In case Lizzy wanted them someday."

Hawk's brow furrowed in a frown. "What kind of things?"

She shrugged. "Little things, the pocket watch you got from your dad, the birthday card you gave me just before you left for deployment." She tried to think back to what she'd tucked away for their daughter. "Oh, and I recently pulled out that packet of information you sent from overseas."

His hand tightened on her knee. "What packet?"

"The brown envelope. You sent it from Afghanistan."

"What was inside?" There was a new sense of urgency in his tone.

"I don't know. You said it was nothing important. That I shouldn't bother opening it and to put it away until you came home."

"And you're certain I sent it to you from Afghanistan?"

"I'm certain that's what you told me when you called." She grew frustrated with his persistence. "Don't you remember sending it to me? Or calling to let me know to expect it?"

"No. I don't." Hawk's clipped tone made her stomach clench. "There are still holes in my memory and I don't recall sending you anything from overseas."

Her stomach clenched with fear. "You think someone else sent it to me?"

He shook his head. "No, I'm sure it was me. I only wish I could remember what it was."

The knots in her stomach tightened. "You should know that I made a call to Fort Bragg during my lunch hour, to let them know I had some stuff of yours they may need. It was probably a lame thing to do, but I was cleaning out the basement and thought maybe the information in the envelope might be important."

"When?" his tone was sharp.

"Earlier this week." She thought back. "Monday or Tuesday. I remember thinking no one would get back to me until after the holidays."

"Did you talk to anyone in particular?"

She shrugged. "The woman who answered the phone said she'd let her superior know. I can't remember her name." She abruptly realized the timing was too much of a coincidence. "You think those men came because of the envelope?"

Hawk glanced over at her. "There's only one way to find out. Once I have you and Lizzy stashed someplace safe, I'll head back to check it out."

Jillian gaped at him. "No! It's too dangerous."

Hawk didn't say anything but she recognized the stubborn glint in his steel blue eyes.

She forced herself to relax. The envelope could be nothing. She'd gotten it over four years ago.

Yet even as Hawk pulled into the parking lot of a drugstore, she couldn't help but hope and pray the brown envelope held the key to getting them all out of danger.

FIVE

Hawk couldn't shake the fact that two men in masks had come to Jillian's home three days after her phone call to Fort Bragg. He realized that his initial assumption had changed. It wasn't his probing into Barton's past that had caused the attack, but Jillian finding the envelope he'd apparently sent more than four years ago.

He absolutely needed to get his hands on the contents of that envelope. But not until he'd made sure Jillian and Lizzy were safe.

He was surprised at how seriously Jillian took the task of caring for his wound. She was a woman on a first aid mission. After purchasing supplies she deemed appropriate, they sat in the front seat of the SUV. She used wipes to wash the front and back of his shoulder, then added antibiotic ointment before placing gauze over the through-and-through bullet wounds.

"We need to get you to a hospital right away." Jillian pinned him with a stern glare. "This will get infected."

"Soon." He knew she was right, but there wasn't time. Not to mention that bullet wounds were an automatic report to the cops, and he wasn't letting that happen. He made a mental note to ask Mitch Callahan if his ER nurse wife, Dana, could get him antibiotics. Enough to hold him over until Jillian and Lizzy were safe.

"I'm hungry," Lizzy said again. "And so is Teddy."

Jillian finished taping the gauze down before turning to her daughter. "I know. The restaurant is right across the street, see?"

Lizzy leaned forward in her car seat. Hawk pulled his T-shirt back on, then shrugged into his leather jacket, hoping the bullet holes marring the smooth leather weren't too obvious. "We'll be there in less than five minutes."

Jillian sat back in her seat and pulled on the seat belt. She placed the garbage from the supplies she'd used neatly in a bag. She was tougher than he remembered, more resilient and independent. It felt weird to have her taking care of him after being alone for so long.

Even with the Callahans, he'd maintained a level of privacy. There were six Callahans in total, and all of them had names starting with the letter M, thanks to a quirk of their parents. Marc was an FBI agent, Miles a homicide detective, Mitch an arson investigator, Matthew a K-9 cop and Maddy an assistant district attorney, while Mike, who was a deputy sheriff now, used to be a private investigator like him. Hawk was closest to Mike but had helped some of the other siblings from time to time over the last couple of years.

Now it was his turn. He decided that after they ate lunch, he'd make the call to Mike asking for as many of the Callahans as were available to meet him at the cabin motel.

The restaurant loomed before him. He passed all the close parking spots to choose one that was behind the building, far enough away that it couldn't be seen from the road.

Satisfied for the moment, he took a few minutes to search for a GPS tracking device. Logically, he felt four armed men with guns wouldn't want a GPS device on their vehicle, but he needed to make sure. Thankfully, he was familiar with this particular SUV make and model, so he knew what he was looking for. He didn't find any type of tracking device, which made him let out a sigh of relief. Still, he'd need a different car and knew the request wouldn't be a surprise to the Callahans.

They'd had a lot of practice hiding from bad guys with guns and had a well-oiled routine.

Jillian took Lizzy out of the car seat and he stepped forward, intending to take the girl from her arms. But then he hesitated, remembering how scared Lizzy was of him and his scarred face.

"Will you let Hawk carry you?" Jillian asked their daughter as if reading his thoughts. "My arms are getting tired."

Lizzy hunched her shoulders, dipping her head shyly, and nodded. Hawk smiled, hoping his expression wasn't too frightening as he gently pulled Lizzy from Jillian's arms.

Lizzy didn't exactly lean against him for support, but she didn't seem upset by being close to him, either. She still had the teddy bear and he was secretly surprised the stuffed animal had made it this far.

He renewed his silent promise to keep Lizzy and Jillian safe from harm.

"You have an ouchie." Lizzy's soft fingers lightly touched his deeply grooved cheek. "Does it hurt?"

It took a minute for him to respond. "No, it doesn't hurt."

"Did your mommy kiss it and make it better?"

This time a genuine smile bloomed on his face. "No, my mommy wasn't there when it happened."

Lizzy studied him intently. "Maybe my mommy could kiss it and make it better."

Jillian let out a choked sound that could have been a horrified gasp or a cough, he wasn't sure which.

"It's okay, Lizzy," he reassured her, wishing he'd gone to see a plastic surgeon to have the scar fixed. Not that he was convinced he'd look all that much better afterward, but it may be enough to be more appealing for his daughter. And, for that matter, to Jillian. "I promise it doesn't hurt."

"Table for three, please," Jillian said to the restaurant hostess.

"Right this way."

Within minutes they were seated at a corner booth that overlooked the main highway. Hawk sat with his back to the wall, facing the door. He mentally mapped out an escape plan as Jillian and Lizzy discussed what they wanted from the menu.

"Would you like to start with something to drink?" Their server, a plump woman whose name tag read Patty, smiled brightly. She had freckles and shockingly red hair that seemed too harsh to be natural. She waited, holding her pen and pad at the ready.

"Coffee for me," Hawk said.

"Me, too," Jillian added. "And chocolate milk for Lizzy, please."

"Coming right up." Patty quickly returned with a pot

of coffee for the adults. The chocolate milk arrived a few minutes later.

They ordered their meals. Burger medium rare for Hawk, turkey club for Jillian and chicken strips with French fries for Lizzy. While they waited for their food to arrive, he pulled out his phone and called Mike.

"Hawk? What's wrong?" The alarm in Mike's tone made him smile.

"I need a favor."

"It must be bad if you're calling in a favor." Mike Callahan knew him too well.

"It is." Hawk watched as Lizzy colored on a paper place mat, with crayons provided by the restaurant to keep children busy. "Meet me at the cabin motel you used last summer with the usual."

Mike let out a low whistle at his request. "The usual being a vehicle, computer and disposable phones."

Hawk rotated his injured shoulder. "Yeah. Also, check with Mitch, see if Dana can get any antibiotics."

"You're wounded?" Mike sounded truly alarmed, as if Hawk being hurt was inconceivable. "What happened? Why didn't you call sooner?"

The corner of Hawk's mouth quirked in a smile. It was nice knowing you had a Callahan covering your back. "Long story. I'll fill you in later."

"Okay, give me an hour, maybe a little longer to get the antibiotics. I don't think Dana can just get them from the hospital without obtaining a prescription."

Hawk's smile faded at the implication. "I don't want her to get in trouble."

"Trust me, Mitch won't let that happen. But we all owe you, Hawk. We'll do our best to get what you need."

"Thank you." Hawk knew it was more than owing

a favor. The Callahans cared about him and wanted to help. It made him realize how much he'd missed being part of a team. Being the lone survivor of the plane crash intended to kill him, he had forged ahead alone. The Thornhills had helped but then hadn't wanted anything more to do with him. Which in hindsight was smart on their part. He'd brought danger to them once, and it was clear they didn't want any further contact that would put them in jeopardy.

He glanced at Jillian, thinking about how he'd lived next door to her for the past five months. Friendly and helpful, yet keeping his distance.

Now he wanted more.

He disconnected from the line and then turned off the phone. He made a mental note to destroy it when they left the restaurant.

Ten minutes later, their meals arrived. Jillian cut up Lizzy's chicken strips and then once again bowed her head to pray. Lizzy was watching him curiously, so he mirrored Jillian's actions, bowing his head and clasping his hands in front of him while she said a whispered prayer.

"Dear Lord, we thank You for keeping us safe in Your care. Please continue to provide us the strength and wisdom we need to seek justice." She paused, then added, "And thank You for this food, too. Amen."

"Amen," Lizzy quipped.

Hawk cleared his throat. "Amen."

Jillian glanced at him in surprise, a pleased expression on her face. "Thanks, Hawk."

He had no idea what she was thanking him for but nodded. "Let's eat. We need to hit the road soon."

She frowned but began to eat her club sandwich. After a few minutes, she asked, "You spoke with Mike?"

"He'll meet us with everything we need." Hawk didn't want to say too much in front of Lizzy. "And he'll stay with you while I go back to your place."

"No. I don't want you to go alone." The stubborn glint was back in her green gaze.

Hawk didn't respond because he wasn't sure how many of the Callahans would be free to come to his aid. If only two brothers were able to come, then he absolutely wanted them both to stay with Jillian and Lizzy. He needed them well protected. If a third was able to come, then he might be able to take someone along for backup.

He desperately needed to get his hands on that envelope. The one he didn't remember sending from Afghanistan. The one Jillian had recently called Fort Bragg about. Hawk had a feeling deep in his gut the contents of the envelope would help him get to the bottom of this mess.

He only hoped and prayed there was evidence in there linking Rick Barton to something illegal.

Because it was clear he couldn't depend on his moldy Swiss-cheese memories.

Jillian was relieved that Hawk had called Mike Callahan for assistance. Not because she didn't trust him, but because she was afraid his wound would soon impact his ability to keep them safe.

Had James ever been as stubborn as Hawk was? Her memories of James were fond and loving, focused on the good times they'd spent together far more than on the bad. They'd met at the restaurant where she'd worked while finishing up her teaching degree. They were only married for a year before James had been deployed and had dated for six months before that. Eighteen months total, another reason that it wasn't easy to mesh the current reality of Hawk with her fading memories of James.

Their marriage hadn't been perfect, no marriage was. Still, she'd mourned a long time for what she'd lost.

Yet James, er, Hawk was sitting beside her.

Lizzy played with her French fries, as if they were tiny dolls who were living in a home together. A tall French fry was telling the smaller one to go clean up her room. "No. Don't want to," Lizzy said in a high, fake voice. "I wanna go outside and play."

"You must clean your room!" The stern taller fry was obviously the mother talking to her child. Jillian's lips curved in a smile.

"Guess there's no daddy French fry," Hawk said in a low voice.

Jillian glanced at him in surprise but then realized that Hawk's keen sense of perception never missed a thing. "Not yet, but that will change once we're able to tell her."

"Tell me what?" Lizzy asked. She popped both the tall French fry and the smaller one into her mouth.

Hawk froze and Jillian could tell their daughter's innocent question, one she had no intention of answering, had shocked him more than any gunshot ever could.

"We wanted to tell you that we're going to another cabin, but this one has a playground." Jillian injected enthusiasm in her tone. "Won't that be fun?"

Lizzy nodded, but her tiny brow puckered in a frown. "Will the bad men find us there?"

A look of horror crossed Hawk's features and then quickly vanished. He reached over and covered her tiny hand with his. "Lizzy, I'm doing everything possible to make sure they'll never find us again."

Lizzy held his gaze for a long, poignant moment. "Okay."

Jillian gave her daughter a quick hug. "Are you finished? We need to leave."

Lizzy bobbed her head up and down. "'Cept, I hav'ta go to the bathroom."

Jillian sensed Hawk's impatience but he didn't say anything. He wasn't used to traveling with young children. So far, Lizzy had taken everything in stride, but it was only a matter of time until she grew cranky. Hawk hadn't seen anything like one of Lizzy's temper tantrums.

It was another ten minutes before she had Lizzy tucked into her car seat and they were back on the road. Hawk didn't say much as he drove, making her wonder what was going through his mind.

James hadn't been afraid to open up to her about his thoughts and feelings. There was a time they'd shared everything.

Yet she also knew that even if her husband hadn't been in a plane crash and left for dead, he probably would have come home from Afghanistan a changed man. In her time at Fort Bragg, other army wives had vented their frustration over the changes in their spouses when they'd come back from being deployed. The moodiness, the quietness, the nightmares.

It was shocking to think that this new version of James, the man she now called Hawk, may have been the same, whether he'd been involved in the plane crash or not.

"What?" Hawk asked, breaking the silence.

She blushed, realizing she'd been staring at him. "Nothing really, just wondering what you were thinking."

He gave a curt nod. "That I should have had plastic surgery to minimize the scar."

She was taken aback by his response. "What? No! I mean, why? That sounds pretty drastic."

Hawk's gaze cut to the rearview mirror to look back at Lizzy before returning to her. "I'm too scary. I don't think telling her the truth now is a good idea."

It was her turn to glance back at their daughter. "She's not afraid of you, Hawk. At least, not anymore."

Hawk's mouth tightened in a grimace. "I'm not sure I believe that. I hate the idea she might be frightened of me."

She lightly touched his forearm. "You need to understand that the day care centers spend a lot of time on their 'Stranger Danger' safety campaign. It's never been about you and your scar but about strangers in general." Jillian knew that her own attitude toward Hawk over these past months hadn't helped. Sure, she'd been grateful for his help and generous support, but she'd never gone out of her way to befriend him, either.

Because of the scar? She didn't want to think so. Hawk was handsome in spite of the scar and she was certain women had let him know how attractive he was during the time they'd been apart.

Hawk dropped his gaze to her left hand. The wedding band she wore felt as if it were burning into her skin.

"It's the same one you gave me," she admitted softly. "I put the diamond away after you...after I got the news, but kept wearing the band."

"Why?"

She hesitated and then told him the truth. "I wanted to save the diamond for Lizzy."

"I meant, why wear the wedding band." Hawk's gravelly voice sent shivers of awareness down her spine.

That was a more complicated answer. "I guess deep down, I still felt married. I wasn't interested in anyone else and wearing the wedding ring kept men away."

There was another long silence. "When I first found you, I thought you'd moved on with someone else. I didn't realize Lizzy was my…" He didn't finish but shrugged and tipped his head back toward their daughter. "I want you to know I wouldn't have blamed you if you had, Jilly. Moved on, I mean."

"Well." She tried to smile. "I guess it's a good thing I didn't."

He looked surprised by her response but didn't say anything more.

Fifteen minutes later, Hawk pulled onto a poorly plowed road, the SUV bouncing from side to side as he navigated between rows of trees. The area was not unlike the wooded landscape surrounding Hawk's cabin. When Hawk brought the vehicle to a stop, Jillian hoped and prayed that this time they wouldn't be forced to flee on foot.

"Stay inside," he said as he pushed open the door on his side. "This won't take long."

She nodded and tried to relax back against the seat. But her nerves were still on edge, and she found herself scanning their surroundings the way Hawk might.

The playground was due west, several yards to her left. The snow wasn't terribly deep and she thought Lizzy might still be able to enjoy the swing set.

Apparently, Hawk need not have worried about there

not being a cabin available this close to the holiday, because he returned a short time later with two keys. "I picked the largest one, across from the playground. Hope that's okay."

"Sounds good to me."

"There are three bedrooms," he added. "One room has twin beds."

The SUV bounced again as he drove toward the large cabin across from the playground. She carried Lizzy inside while Hawk unlatched the car seat and brought that in with them.

"We're not keeping the car?" she guessed.

"No." He frowned as he took note of Lizzy's footie pajamas. "I should have asked Mike to bring clothes and stuff for Lizzy. I'll pick some things up on my way back from your place."

"Yeah, well, about that." She cleared her throat as Lizzy ran into the living room. "I forgot to tell you something important."

His gaze narrowed. "Like what?"

"Mommy! I wanna watch TV!"

"I'll be right back." Jillian went into the living room, found the remote and searched for a cartoon channel. When Lizzy was satisfied, she returned to the kitchen. Hawk didn't move, his arms crossed over his chest, his expression forbidding.

She held up a hand as if to ward off an argument. "I forgot to mention the envelope isn't at home."

"Where is it?"

She grimaced. "I left it on my desk at school. The last day before the holiday break is so chaotic—we had a party, then did a Christmas program for the parents. I completely forgot about it."

"At school." Hawk's shoulders relaxed. "Okay, you can tell me where your classroom is and I'll find it."

It was her turn to cross her arms over her chest. "It's better if I go with you."

"No."

The single word made her cheeks flush with anger. "Yes. The place is closed for the holiday break. And you won't know which key to use. Besides, with me being there, we'll be in and out in a heartbeat."

Hawk held her gaze for several long moments, clearly not happy. He turned away without saying a word.

She told herself she didn't care if he was upset with her. The school was locked down and so was her classroom. Sending Hawk in alone seemed wrong. That was her space.

They needed to work together on this, but it was clear Hawk would rather operate alone.

Did that extend to his personal life, too? He claimed he hadn't told her the truth about who he was because he thought she'd moved on, but she wasn't buying it. There had been many opportunities for him to have casually asked questions about her life, about Lizzy, but he hadn't.

She sensed Hawk would rather live alone in a house than be a part of the family with her and Lizzy.

And that knowledge cut deep.

SIX

Hawk stood at the window overlooking the playground, clenching his jaw so tight he feared he'd crack a few molars. He couldn't remember ever being this angry with Jillian before. Why in the world would she place herself in danger? She needed to be safe. If anything happened to Jillian, who would take care of Lizzy?

A cold fist squeezed his heart. He was the only one who should be facing danger. Not Jillian. She and Lizzy were innocent.

He tried to relax his jaw to think about the situation logically.

Sneaking into Brookland Elementary might not be the highest risk situation they'd face. Not as bad as being trailed through the woods by four armed men. But her assistance wasn't necessary.

He much preferred going alone.

Several moments later, Jillian left the kitchen, and her muted voice talking to Lizzy reached him from the living room. He wanted to join them but forced himself to stay where he was. He also wanted to call Mike to get an ETA, but he'd crushed his cell phone and Jillian's with the heel of his boot and dumped them in the trash outside the family restaurant while Jillian and Lizzy were in the restroom.

Normally he prided himself on being patient. It was the hallmark of a good special ops soldier. Blowing out a heavy sigh, he began to formulate a strategy for once the Callahans arrived. He needed more information on Barton but didn't want to place Mike or his brothers in the senator's crosshairs. But he also needed to get into the elementary school for the envelope that may hold the evidence he needed to fill some of the holes in his memory.

His body tensed when he saw a black SUV pulling up. Upon recognizing Mike's familiar face behind the wheel, he went out to meet him.

"Hey," Mike acknowledged as he slid out from behind the wheel and tossed the keys toward him. Hawk caught them in the air. "This is your new ride. Noah is on the way, and Matt said he and Duchess would be able to help out, too."

"Thanks." Hawk was humbled by the response. Noah Sinclair was married to Maddy, the only female of the Callahan siblings. Noah was a cop. So was Matt Callahan, and Duchess was Matt's K-9 partner, a large black-and-tan German shepherd.

"Oh, and Dana was able to get the antibiotics you requested," Mike continued. "She hit up one of her ER physician friends who agreed to write the prescription as long as you come in to be seen in the next few days."

That wasn't going to happen until they managed to get to the bottom of this mess, but he let it go. The throbbing in his wounded shoulder had become more intense over the past hour, and he hoped the antibiotics would help control the potential infection brewing there.

Mike thrust a bag at him. "Take the antibiotics, make

sure you drink a lot of fluids, then get the phones activated so we have a way to contact you. I need you to fill me in."

Hawk nodded and carried the supplies inside. He downed the antibiotic and went to work on the phones, then turned his attention to the computer. Mike joined him at the table at the same time Jillian came over to see what they were doing.

"Hi. I'm Jillian Wade," she introduced herself to Mike.

"Mike Callahan." Mike rose to his feet and offered his hand.

Hawk had to stop himself from jumping up and stepping between them. A ridiculous response, as Mike was happily married to Shayla and a doting father to their son, Brodie.

He really needed to get a grip. Jillian didn't belong to him anymore. James was dead. He was Hawk now.

"Nice to meet you," Jillian said warmly. "Glad you're here to help. We can use it."

"Yeah, so, how do you know Hawk, anyway?" Mike's curious gaze annoyed him.

"We're next-door neighbors." Jillian gestured toward Hawk. "And when two armed men showed up at my house with guns, Hawk saved our lives."

"Our lives?" Mike questioned.

"Me and my daughter, Lizzy," Jillian said, jerking her thumb toward the living room, from where the sound of cartoons could be heard. "She's four."

"I have a four-year-old son, too." Mike beamed. "Brodie is a great kid."

Hawk was getting tired of the small talk. He didn't do chitchat and didn't see the point. "Can we get back on task here? Talk about the men with guns?"

Mike's expression turned serious. "What do you know about them?"

"Only that they're professionals," Hawk admitted. "Likely with military training, but not Special Forces."

"Why not Special Forces?" Jillian asked.

Hawk shifted in his seat, uncomfortable talking with her about this. If he had his way, he'd shield her and Lizzy from all the bad things that happened in life. "Because I was able to take them both out without a problem. They made mistakes and I capitalized on them."

Jillian held his gaze for a long moment. "Could be you're just a better Special Forces guy than they were. You did that with the four men who tracked us to the cabin, too."

"Four men?" Mike whistled under his breath. "Who did you anger?"

"Fair question." Hawk gestured toward the computer, where he'd brought up the image of the man he suspected was behind all of this. "What do you know about Senator Barton?"

Mike squinted at the screen. "Not much, but I'm willing to dig into his background for you."

"Maybe later." Hawk couldn't help wanting to protect one of the few friends he had.

"Why don't you start at the beginning?" Jillian suggested. "Telling Mike half a story isn't going to help. He needs to hear everything, going back to your deployment in Afghanistan, through the plane crash and the recent events."

She was right. Hawk glanced at his watch. It was after one in the afternoon, and he knew they shouldn't use the key to enter the elementary school until after dusk had fallen.

As briefly as possible, he told Mike about his deployment as a special ops soldier, how his team had died in the Appalachian Mountains and his subsequent memory loss and survival against the odds. Mike listened intently, without interruption. When Hawk got to the part about Jillian being his wife and the information he'd sent, Mike's gaze widened in surprise, at the relationship as much as at the information.

"So Jillian calls Fort Bragg about this envelope and within days a two-man team breaks into her house." Mike let out a snort of derision. "That's no coincidence."

"Agreed. And the two-man team turned into a four-man team at the cabin." Hawk gently massaged his injured shoulder. "I was able to take them down, but only put one of them out of commission permanently."

Mike grimaced, understanding how difficult their escape had been. "Impressive that you were able to get away safely, although maybe I should ask Dana to come out here to look at your shoulder."

"It's fine."

Mike rolled his eyes and glanced back at the face on the computer screen. "And you think this is all related to Senator Rick Barton?"

Hawk nodded. "I know he was a major in the army while I was overseas. Heck, he bragged about his military background while running for office last year. I have a snippet of memory of him standing and talking to someone else while deep in the Afghan mountains. But other than a sense of horror and wrongdoing, I have no idea what that bit of memory means. I have to think he was in a place he wouldn't normally be. From what I remember of Afghanistan, officers didn't go into the mountains on their own. Not without a special ops team."

Mike pursed his lips thoughtfully. "Yeah, I get that. Officers are usually calling the shots, directing the team about what to do... Not off somewhere on their own."

"Exactly," Hawk said. "And I also discovered that Todd Hayes, who's the current secretary of defense, was stationed in Afghanistan as well. The two of them being overseas and now in Washington seems too much of a coincidence."

"Agreed. Seems logical to get the envelope first and see if there's something inside that will provide a clue." Mike shrugged. "I propose that once Matt and Noah get here, you and I hit the road, leaving the two of them and Duchess to watch over Jillian and Lizzy."

"No, I'm going with you," Jillian said before Hawk could respond. "I have a key to the school and my classroom. I know where I left the folder and this will all go more smoothly if you take me along."

To his credit, Mike didn't respond but glanced at Hawk. "Your call."

"No, it's my call," Jillian interjected, a sharp edge to her tone. "I'm serious about this. If we get caught, I have a good reason to be in the school, you don't."

Hawk tried to come up with logical response that would convince her to stay behind, but he sensed it was useless.

Jillian would continue to insist on going along, and he didn't have a good way to stop her, short of physically restraining her.

"Fine," he finally agreed. "You can come with us, but you need to promise to follow orders without question." He narrowed his eyes. "Your life and ours will depend on that."

Jillian didn't hesitate. "I promise. And thank you."

"Don't thank me." Hawk couldn't hide the frustration in his tone. "The only other option is to tie you to the chair and take the keys from you by force."

She simply raised a brow. "You would never hurt me."

No, he wouldn't. She was his weakness, which was exactly why he didn't want her accompanying him. If more armed men showed up and used Jillian or Lizzy as leverage, he'd fold like a lawn chair.

Mike hid a grin and Hawk knew that his buddy was enjoying this, far too much.

It wasn't that long ago that the situation was reversed. Mike was protecting his wife, Shayla, and his son, Brodie. Shayla had been stubborn back then, too.

They'd managed to survive, breaking open the case surrounding Mike's father's murder without anyone getting seriously injured.

Hawk could only hope and pray that this situation would turn out the same way.

He couldn't imagine a future without Jillian and Lizzy in it.

Jillian did her best not to let Hawk know how much his attitude toward her coming along to get the envelope stung, but it wasn't easy.

"Mommy! I don't wanna wear my pajamas anymore."

She went into the living room to find Lizzy unzipping her footie pajamas. "Honey, we don't have anything else for you to wear, so you need to keep your pajamas on."

Lizzy's lower lip trembled. "I wanna wear my pink leggings."

They were her favorite, Jillian knew, but there was nothing she could do to fix it.

"We can stop to pick up some stuff for her on our

way back," Hawk offered. "I don't blame her for wanting something else to wear."

"Pink leggings," Lizzy repeated, gazing up at Hawk as if he'd given her the world instead of a change of clothes. "With a flowery skirt on top."

"Pink leggings and flowery skirt," Hawk repeated. "Got it."

"Maybe something Christmassy, too," Jillian suggested.

Lizzy nodded and excitedly hopped from one foot to the other. "I wanna look like an angel, like in the Christmas program."

"I'll do my best," Jillian promised. It made her feel better to have another reason to go with Hawk to Brookland Elementary. She doubted Hawk had a clue how to shop for a four-year-old.

"Maybe we should leave early, stop at the store along the way," Hawk suggested.

"Fine with me." She knew her voice was cool but didn't care.

Moments later the sound of an approaching car had both Hawk and Mike heading over to the door. She stayed by Lizzy, only relaxing once the two men put their respective weapons away and greeted the newcomers.

"Come on Lizzy." She took her daughter by the hand. "Do you want to meet the doggie?"

"Yes!" Lizzy ran into the kitchen but stopped abruptly when she realized Duchess was at eye level. "Big doggie."

"Duchess, friend." A man who looked similar to Mike placed his hand on Lizzy's head. "Friend," he repeated.

"Scary big doggie," Lizzy said, huddling close to Jillian's legs.

"She's very friendly, Lizzy," he said with a smile. "Hold out your hand and let Duchess give it a little sniff."

Lizzy held out her hand, and Duchess lowered her nose and took in the little girl's scent. Then Duchess licked Lizzy's fingers, making her laugh. Lizzy stroked the dog's fur and Duchess licked her again.

Lizzy ran back into the living room with Duchess on her heels. Jillian was reassured by how well Duchess interacted with her daughter and knew Lizzy would be unrelenting in her demand for a puppy of her own, after this.

Hawk introduced her to Noah and Matt, then got down to business. "I need you two to stay here with Lizzy while we head back to Brookland," he instructed. "Shouldn't take us longer than two hours to get there, find the envelope, stop to pick up a few things and get back."

Noah and Matt nodded in agreement. Matt asked, "Anything we can do while we're here?"

Jillian saw the indecision in Hawk's blue eyes.

"We need to dig into Senator Barton's background," Mike said when Hawk remained silent.

"It may be too dangerous. I'll do it when I get back," Hawk quickly interjected.

"We have time," Noah said. "May as well be productive."

"Don't worry, Hawk." Mike clapped him on his injured shoulder, making Hawk wince. "We can handle the heat."

The last bit of anger Jillian had been clinging to instantly evaporated. Hawk wasn't just being overly protective of her but of his friends, as well. He didn't want any of the Callahans or their brother-in-law to be in danger from investigating the senator.

The time he'd spent surviving on his own in the Appalachian Mountains must have really changed him.

"The computer can't be traced to us," Matt added. "We'll be fine. As long as Lizzy accepts us being here with her."

"Duchess has already won her over," Jillian said with a smile. "I think she'll be fine."

"We'll bring dinner back with us," Mike said, glancing around the kitchen. "That way we can continue working without interruption."

Hawk appeared to be resigned to the arrangements. "Let's go, then. We have a lot to do."

Before they got into Mike's SUV, Mike and Hawk smeared mud over the front and back license plates. She assumed that was to make it difficult for anyone to trace the vehicle to them.

The ride to Brookland seemed to take forever. Jillian rode up front as Hawk drove, but the two men kept up a stream of conversation that centered around Mike's new job, the rest of the Callahans and other things she didn't know anything about.

When they passed a store that carried both children's clothes and toys, Jillian tapped Hawk's arm. "Let's stop there, first."

"Sure." He pulled into the parking lot and found a parking space. They were all out in the open so there was no way to hide their vehicle.

Inside the store, Jillian quickly headed for the children's clothing section. It didn't take long to pull out two outfits for Lizzy, the pink leggings with a flowery skirt that she'd requested and a green-and-red one with a Santa elf on the front. She hoped the elf would be okay in lieu of an angel.

"Size 4T," Hawk murmured, peering at the tag. "What does that mean?"

"Four Toddler," Jillian and Mike replied at the same time.

Hawk still looked confused but let it go. A toy display was strategically placed near the children's clothing. Hawk picked up a box containing a doll wearing a puffy gold dress and held it out to her. "Do you think Lizzy would like this?"

She was touched by his question. "She'd love it."

"Good." He tucked the doll dressed in gold into the cart beside the two outfits. "Do you need anything, Jillian?"

Her cheeks went warm and she quickly shook her head. "Maybe some groceries for breakfast and lunch."

They bought the basics, which Jillian sensed was more than Hawk had anticipated, then headed over to the shortest checkout lane. Hawk insisted on paying with cash, and soon they were back on the road. Dusk was falling early as it was the shortest day of the year.

Jillian provided directions to Brookland Elementary. Hawk pulled into a parking spot near the front door and shut down the engine.

"Ready?" he asked.

She nodded and pulled the keys out of her coat pocket. As she approached the door, she sucked in a harsh breath.

The door wasn't locked, the mechanism clearly having been broken.

"Get behind me," Hawk said in a low tone as he pulled out his gun. "Mike, cover from behind."

"On it."

They carefully entered the building. Jillian was glad to see that the main school corridor looked the same as it had when she'd left the previous day, which seemed like a week ago rather than just over twenty-four hours.

But when they approached her classroom, they found the door handle was broken there, too. And when she pushed open the door, she saw the classroom was a disaster.

Desks were turned over, their contents spilling over the floor.

"They found the folder before we did," Hawk said in a resigned tone.

Jillian stepped closer to her desk. Every drawer had been opened, and the three-ring binder containing her lesson plans that she'd left on her desk was lying on the floor.

She picked it up, flipping to the back pocket.

The brown envelope was still there, tucked inside. The assailants who'd ransacked the place had missed it! She took it out and handed it to Hawk. He looked at her name written in his handwriting from over four years ago, and then opened it up.

"Photos," he said, an edge of excitement in his voice. "We have what we need, let's go."

Jillian was happy to leave, although she felt she needed to report the school break-in to the police.

As they headed outside and climbed back in the SUV, the sound of gunfire rang out.

Hawk hit the gas and drove like a maniac out of the parking lot.

They'd been found!

SEVEN

The back wheels of the SUV fishtailed as Hawk took a hard left out of the parking lot in a desperate attempt to ditch the gunmen. He couldn't afford to assume there was only one gunman: there may very well be another one stationed along the single road leading away from the school.

"Get down." He pushed Jillian's head toward her lap. He needed to get away. Instincts had him making a quick right, then right again, then left.

Jillian was murmuring something that sounded like a prayer. Hawk continued to make random turns, doing his best to get far away from the school without being tailed. As he drove, he was grateful for Mike's idea of putting mud over the license plates.

Mike had opened one of the back windows and was peering behind them, with his gun held ready.

"See anyone following us?" Hawk asked.

"Negative."

It was good news, but he couldn't afford to assume they were safe. Not yet.

Maybe not ever.

Five tense minutes passed. Hawk concentrated on putting distance between them and the school while Mike kept his gaze on their tail. The interior of the SUV grew cold, but Hawk ignored the discomfort.

After a total of fifteen minutes passed, Mike sat back in his seat and rolled up the window. "We're clear."

Hawk nodded but continued to keep one eye on the rearview mirror just in case. He couldn't afford to be caught off guard again.

Jillian sat up, pushing her red hair out of her face. "God has been watching over us," she said softly.

"Amen," Mike agreed.

Hawk wasn't sure how to respond. Despite the holes in his memory, he could remember a moment he'd sat in church with Jillian, but it had been so long ago. Before his deployment to Afghanistan. Before he'd caught a glimpse of Rick Barton in the Afghan mountains.

Before their plane had crashed into the Appalachian Mountains, killing everyone on board except for him.

Knowing that Jillian and Mike had maintained their faith made him wonder if he'd given up too soon.

Was it possible that God had been watching over him for the past five years?

He shrugged the thought aside and focused on getting back to the cabin motel without taking a direct route. In fact, he'd gone further east than he'd intended, so he took a left and headed north for a bit, before turning again to head west.

"Don't forget we need to bring dinner back," Mike spoke up from the back seat.

Hawk nodded. "Let me know what you want."

"Jillian, what do you think? We need something that Lizzy will like, too," Mike said.

Hawk mentally kicked himself for momentarily forgetting about Lizzy. Being a father, Mike had automatically remembered they were feeding a child. Hawk needed to remember he had a daughter. He cleared his throat, awkwardly. "Whatever Lizzy and Jillian want is fine with me."

"How about pizza?" Jillian offered. "We can get a small cheese pizza for me and Lizzy, and a large loaded with everything for you guys."

"Works for me," Mike said. "Okay with you, Hawk?"

"Sure." Hawk wasn't concerned about food, although the antibiotic was making his stomach feel queasy. He was preoccupied with how the gunmen had gone to the school to find the envelope, which meant they'd traced Jillian's call. Had they gone to the school prior to sneaking into her house? It made sense, but while he felt certain that had been the sequence of events, there was no way to know for sure.

At least they still had the envelope. He'd only taken a quick glance at the two photos inside and had been disappointed not to see Rick Barton's familiar face. He'd have to take a closer look to see if he recognized who the guy was and whether there was something incriminating in them.

There must be, or the senator wouldn't have sent men wearing ski masks with guns to get it.

"There's a pizza place up ahead," Mike said, tapping him on the shoulder. "We're only about ten minutes from the cabin motel, so it's a good place to stop."

Hawk grunted in agreement. The next exit was three miles away, and he took the exit, keeping a wary eye on the road behind them.

As darkness had fallen, it became increasingly difficult to keep track of a tail. Headlights came and went,

some round, some square, but it was almost impossible
to tell makes or models of the vehicles they belonged to.

No cars followed him off the interstate. He dug in his
pocket for money to pay for the pizza, but Mike waved
him off. "Stay here, I'll get them."

The door shut behind Mike, leaving him with Jillian.
He glanced at her, trying to think of something to say.

She lifted a weary hand. "Don't say it. I already
know you were right. I shouldn't have insisted on coming along."

"That wasn't what I was going to say," he protested.
"It's true I hate putting you in danger, but I have to admit
that if you hadn't been there, we may not have found the
envelope."

There was a brief silence before she asked, "Do you
think they wrecked my house, too?"

Although he wanted to protect her, he couldn't bring
himself to lie. "Yes, I believe they searched your house,
too. Why stop at the school and not go all the way? It's
probably the first thing they did after we left."

Jillian looked as if she might cry but then surprised
him by muttering, "Those rotten jerks."

"Yeah." He wished he had the right to pull her into
his arms to offer comfort. Regardless of the fact that the
gunmen had followed the envelope to Jillian's home and
school, it was only because he'd sent it to her.

Why would he do such a thing? It went against his na-
ture to put his wife in danger. Although he hadn't known
about Lizzy, but still…

Then again, he hadn't anticipated being in a plane
crash, either. It must have been right after he'd seen Barton in the mountains that he'd sent her the photos. Right

after they'd been told they were being put on a plane to Washington, DC, to be debriefed.

And it had sat dormant all this time. Until Jillian had decided to clean out the box of his stuff.

"I hope the photos are helpful," Jillian said, breaking into his thoughts.

"Me, too." He thought about pulling them out now but caught sight of Mike heading toward the SUV carrying two large boxes of pizza.

"That didn't take long," Jillian said, glancing back at Mike as he slid in behind Hawk.

"Nope." Mike grinned and patted the boxes. "I got two large pizzas, one with half cheese and half with the works. I figure the guys will be hungry."

"Good plan," Jillian agreed.

Hawk started the SUV and drove out of the parking lot. Instead of heading immediately west, he took the ramp going on the opposite direction. He sensed Jillian eyeing him curiously, but she didn't say anything.

After five miles, he got off the interstate and took a highway headed south. He knew from previous trips that the highway would eventually take them to the cabin motel. It was longer, but worth the effort to make sure they weren't followed.

"Must be the scenic route," Mike commented from the back seat.

"Yep." The tantalizing scent of pizza sauce and cheese made his mouth water. "Won't take much longer."

"Hey, I've got the food back here, I won't starve," Mike joked.

"Save some for Lizzy," Jillian admonished him.

Their banter was an effort to lighten the somber mood. Hawk appreciated it but couldn't shake the memory of the close call. He needed to find a way to stay one step ahead of these guys, since the senator had more money and resources than they did.

When they reached the cabin motel, the pizza was greeted with enthusiasm. Jillian took the bag of clothes they'd bought for Lizzy and quickly took her daughter into the bedroom to change. It wouldn't be long before she'd need to put her jammies on again, but that didn't seem to matter. When Lizzy came out wearing the pink leggings and holding the doll in her arms, his heart thumped crazily in his chest.

"Thank you, Mr. Hawk." From the way she said that, he knew she must have been prompted by Jillian.

"You're very welcome," he managed in his usual hoarse voice. He longed to take his daughter in his arms but knew it was too soon.

At least she wasn't crying at the mere sight of him.

"Are you hungry?" Jillian asked, putting a pillow on the kitchen chair so Lizzy could reach the table.

"Yes," Lizzy agreed, holding the doll in one hand while trying to climb into the chair with the other.

"Let's put Belle over here, shall we?" Jillian suggested. "We don't want her to get messy."

"Okay." Lizzy was content to have her doll placed in the living room.

"Let's say grace," Mike suggested.

Hawk wasn't surprised and took note of how Jillian eagerly participated in the brief prayer.

As the others dug into the pizza, he took a moment to pull the two photos out of the brown envelope. The top one was a clear view of a soldier meeting with a man who looked to be an insurgent, based on how he was dressed and the AK-47 he cradled in his arms.

The second photo was even more interesting. It was a close-up photo of an open box of guns. Hawk shifted his gaze from one photo to the next. The box was on the ground near the two men, the American soldier and the unknown rebel.

He sat back in his chair for a long moment, the implication reeling in his mind. Was it possible he'd witnessed a gun sale between one of the men he'd fought alongside and the enemy?

And if so, how did Senator Barton fit into the puzzle? He had to assume this was the reason he and his team had been targeted.

Because they'd seen too much.

Safe in the cabin, Jillian tried to put those moments that they'd been under fire out of her mind. Focusing on Lizzy helped and she silently promised herself that next time, she'd listen to Hawk.

If she and Hawk hadn't escaped today, what would have happened to Lizzy? With no surviving relatives, their daughter would no doubt end up in the foster care system.

She was thankful that God had kept them safe, but she also knew that her insistence on going along with Hawk and Mike could have ended far differently.

Her stomach unknotted enough that she was able to eat two slices of pizza. Watching Hawk, she noticed that he'd pulled out the photos from the envelope and was studying them carefully. Before she could ask him about them, Mike did.

"Something interesting?" Mike asked.

Hawk nodded. "Yeah. I think I know why I've been targeted."

"Why is that?" Noah asked.

Hawk slid the photos across the table toward the others. "Take a look, tell me what you see."

Jillian leaned over to see for herself, but the glare on the photo made it difficult to see the details.

"Mommy, I'm done," Lizzy announced.

"Okay." She stood and went over to get a wet napkin to wipe off the tomato sauce and cheese from her daughter's hands and face, before setting her down. "Don't forget Belle."

"I won't." Lizzy scampered over to pick up her doll and began to play in the living room.

"One of our guys sold guns to an insurgent?" Noah asked, his tone reflecting his horror.

"That's what I see," Hawk agreed, his expression grim. "Who is this guy? Other than being an American soldier?"

Jillian could barely comprehend what they were saying. "You mean, one of our men sold the enemy guns for money?"

"That dirtbag" Mike said harshly. "To put American guns in the hands of the insurgents is beyond awful. How many of our men and women died being shot by American guns wielded by the enemy?"

"Too many," Matt said quietly. "No wonder Senator Barton has sent armed men after you."

"Yeah, except there's no way to prove Barton was involved," Hawk said.

Jillian's stomach knotted up all over again. Holding onto the photos felt like holding onto a stick of dynamite. The whole thing could blow up in their faces at any time.

"Maybe we should send it to the newspapers," Mike

suggested. "Going public may be the best way to protect you and your family."

Hawk grimaced. "My word and a grainy picture of a guy I can't identify? That won't get me very far." He paused, then added, "Besides, even if I could prove this soldier is linked to Barton, the situation could be taken out of context and turned the other way. Barton could claim the guy was an insurgent informant who returned the box of stolen guns to the US."

There was a long moment of silence as they imagined how that scenario would play out.

"What if we can find other evidence?" Noah suggested. "Something that would link Barton to the guns?"

"You mean like serial numbers?" Hawk shook his head. "Too many years have passed to track them down."

"Are we sure Senator Barton is involved?" She asked. "It's a serious allegation against a powerful man."

There was a long moment before Hawk spoke up. "I believe Senator Barton is involved, because I have a clear memory of seeing him in the Afghan mountains." He pointed to the photo on the table. "Just like this."

"But that guy isn't Barton," Noah said, stating the obvious.

"I know." Hawk's expression went hard. "But don't you see? Whoever this guy in the photo is, he must have friends in high places. They rigged my team's plane to crash in the mountains."

"True," Mike said, trying to appease Hawk. "So let's say Barton is involved. Maybe it's about money and power. Could be Barton has always aspired to be elected into office. What if we tried to trace the money?" Mike gestured toward the computer. "Digging into his campaign funds may reveal something interesting."

"Again, this was all five years ago." Hawk abruptly stood, revealing his frustration. "Anything that far back will be well covered up by now."

"We don't know that until we look," Mike said.

Hawk shook his head. "It's impossible. My family won't be safe until we can find proof that links Barton to the guns."

"Hawk," Mike began, but it was too late. Hawk strode out of the kitchen, walked through the living room and disappeared into one of the bedrooms.

Leaving a tense silence in his wake.

The Callahans looked at each other, then at her. "Don't worry," Mike said in an attempt to be helpful. "We'll figure this out."

Jillian tried to summon a smile, but inside she felt an overwhelming sense of dread. Until now, Hawk had been her pillar of strength.

His lack of faith was like taking a sledgehammer to the foundation of her fragile home.

"Excuse me," she managed as she rose to her feet. She followed Hawk's path through the living room, making sure Lizzy was okay, before she lightly rapped on the bedroom door.

There was no answer, but that didn't stop her from opening the door a bit. "Hawk?"

She could see his dark silhouette standing in front of the window, the moonlight reflecting over the lingering patches of snow. She pushed the door open further and went inside.

Jillian was torn between offering comfort and demanding he find a way to keep Lizzy safe.

"I'm sorry." His hoarse voice was low and rough. "I

never should have survived that mountain crash. And I never, ever should have mailed those photos to you."

"Hawk, please. It hurts me when you say things like that." She tentatively approached, resting her hand on his back. His muscles went tense beneath her touch, and she feared he'd pull away from her. "I'm glad you survived the crash. And I'm grateful to have you here with me now."

For a long moment he didn't move, but then he slowly turned to face her.

She stared up at him, searching his expression in the moonlight. Then she lifted her hand and cupped his scarred cheek. He flinched and tried to move away, but she held firm. "Please don't lose faith," she whispered.

"Jilly…" Her name was little more than a sigh. He slowly placed his hands on her waist and drew her close. She slipped her hand around his neck and pulled his head down so she could kiss him.

His mouth on hers was familiar yet different. The chemistry between them had always sizzled, but there was also a newness to the embrace. And when they finally came up for air, she felt more confused than ever, unable to fully mesh the Hawk she was with now to the man she'd once married.

EIGHT

Hawk had no idea how it happened. One minute he was beating himself up inside for being so stupid as to bring danger to the two people he loved most in the world, and the next he was kissing Jilly as if he'd never stop.

"I—um," he fumbled for what to say, sensing an apology would not be welcome. He may have holes in his memory surrounding the past, but right here, right now, was crystal clear in his mind.

Jilly had kissed him. She'd put her hand on his scarred cheek, refusing to let him pull away, and had kissed him. He found it hard to imagine she wasn't repulsed by his scarred face.

He'd held his wife in his arms for the first time in five years, and now that he had, he realized how much he didn't want to let her go.

Yet even while he silently rejoiced over their kiss and embrace, he warned himself not to read too much into what had transpired between them. They were on the run and in danger. Emotions were always heightened in times of stress.

James was gone, and only Hawk remained. He refused to hold Jillian to vows they'd exchanged what seemed like a lifetime ago.

Even as all these thoughts tumbled through his mind, he couldn't imagine his life without Jillian and Lizzy.

His wife and daughter.

"Hawk, I know you've been through a lot, but you can't give up. I need you to be strong." She paused and added, "Lizzy and I both need you to stay strong and focused. There has to be something we can do to reveal the truth about what happened five years ago."

"I'm not giving up," he assured her, regretting his moment of weakness. He'd stared at the photos, willing his memory to return, but the gaps had stubbornly remained. He remembered Jilly, the brief moment he'd seen Barton in the mountains, but not the identity of the soldier in the photo. He shook off the depressing thoughts. "I promise I won't rest until you and Lizzy are safe."

"I believe you. And remember, we're in this together," she said, reaching for his hand.

It was on the tip of his tongue to point out that her only job was to keep Lizzy safe, but he didn't want to ruin the moment. Instead he gave her hand a squeeze before letting go and moving back toward the living room.

"Mommy, look! Belle is on TV!" Lizzy pointed excitedly at the television screen as she clutched her doll to her chest. "Isn't she beautiful?"

"Not as pretty as you," Jilly said with a smile, dropping a kiss on top of their daughter's head.

Hawk was secretly pleased his gift had made Lizzy happy. Sure, one doll couldn't make up for missing the past four years of her life, but it was a start to forging a relationship of some sort with his daughter.

"I found it on the kids' channel," Mike offered. "Figured she'd love seeing it."

"Thank you, Mike." The way Jilly smiled at Mike

made Hawk grind his teeth together to keep him from saying something stupid. Mike was hardly a threat; the guy was head over heels in love with his wife. There was no reason for Hawk to act like a jealous fool.

"Mr. Hawk, will you watch Belle with me?" Lizzy asked, looking up at him with a shy smile.

Hawk's heart melted and he knew he'd do anything to keep his daughter happy. "Sure, for a few minutes."

He dropped down beside her on the sofa, watching Lizzy more than the cartoon on the television. Her joy made him smile. Lizzy clapped her hands, dragging his attention to the television. He had no idea there was a whole movie about the doll he'd picked up on impulse at the store, but apparently his instinct had been right on.

It took him a minute to realize the movie Lizzy was watching was *Beauty and the Beast*. Belle was Beauty, and the interaction between Belle and the Beast reminded him too much of his new relationship with Jilly.

Only he knew his physical handicap wouldn't change after a kiss and declaration of love.

"Hawk, do you have a minute?" Mike called from the kitchen.

With reluctance, he left his daughter's side and crossed over to join them.

"Remember Ryker Tillman?"

Hawk nodded. He'd met the soldier six months ago, when they'd all worked together with Mike and the rest of the Callahans to uncover the truth about an organization known as the Dark Knights, who were responsible for former Milwaukee Police Chief Max Callahan's murder. "What about him?"

"I just spoke to Ryker. He's busy now, but he agreed to head up here tomorrow to help us identify this guy."

Mike tapped the photo. "Maybe once we know who this guy is, we'll be able to find the link to Barton."

The possibility sparked a glimmer of hope. "That would be great."

"Listen, we need to hit the road," Matt said. "But we'll return in the morning."

Hawk wanted to protest but understood the Callahans and Noah all had wives and kids waiting at home. "Thanks."

The men pulled on their jackets and headed outside.

Hawk walked with them, watching as they split up. Mike headed toward the SUV that Hawk had stolen from the masked men. They'd run the plate but it was only registered to a corporation, not an individual. The corp was called Maxwell, Inc. and didn't sound familiar. The plan was to abandon it near the lakefront, in the complete opposite direction from where the cabin motels were located.

Matt and Noah would follow in the vehicle they had arrived in, picking up Mike and taking him home.

When they were gone, Hawk made a final sweep of the area outside the cabin, familiarizing himself with the terrain, before going back inside.

In the living room, he could hear Jillian telling Lizzy to get ready for bed now that the movie was over.

He sat in front of the computer, staring morosely at the picture of Senator Rick Barton on the screen.

Was Jillian right? What if Barton wasn't involved? Was Hawk being foolish to trust a five-year-old memory fragment? After everything he'd been through, there was no doubt his mind could easily play tricks on him.

He pulled up the search function with a renewed sense of steely determination. The memory was real. Jillian had proved real, and so was what he'd seen that day in Afghanistan. He couldn't believe otherwise.

Which meant there had to be proof somewhere of Barton being involved in dirty dealings.

He just had to find it.

Jillian tossed and turned on her twin bed next to Lizzy's, the memory of Hawk's kiss making it impossible to sleep.

When he'd pulled away, she'd thought for sure he was going to apologize for kissing her despite the fact that *she* was the one who'd kissed *him*.

Kissed Hawk, not James. Weird how the two men had become separate in her mind. It wasn't the scar that grooved his cheek that made him different, but more the man he'd become.

Maybe because her memories of James were pre-Lizzy, pre-deployment. The reality of Hawk helping her escape the gunmen in her home, in the woods outside his cabin, and again outside the elementary school, was very different.

Caring for Hawk felt like a betrayal to James. Those years after she'd been told James had died, she'd mourned what they'd lost. The chance to be a family.

Yet now that Hawk was here, alive and well, she still hadn't told Lizzy he was her father.

She must have fallen asleep at some point, because the enticing scent of fresh brewed coffee woke her up the following morning.

Peering over at the bed on the other side of the wall, she could see Lizzy was still asleep. Moving as silently as possible, Jillian slid out of bed and made her way to the door. She opened it just enough to slip through, then closed it behind her.

Hawk was in the kitchen, his dark hair damp from a recent washing. She put a hand to her tousled auburn hair and wished she'd taken the time to find the brush she'd purchased for Lizzy.

"Good morning," she greeted him as she came into the kitchen. "I hope you didn't shower with that wounded shoulder."

Hawk glanced at her, his blue eyes intense. "Morning. And no, I didn't. Are you hungry? I was about to make eggs but wasn't sure how you and Lizzy preferred to have them cooked."

She was surprised he didn't remember she liked her eggs over easy while he always made his own sunny-side up. "Lizzy likes them scrambled."

"And you?"

"Over easy." She crossed over to the coffeepot and filled a mug. He pushed the carton of milk toward her and then opened the cupboard to pull down a small container of sugar.

"Thanks." She added the milk and sugar to her coffee and then took a seat at the table, putting distance between them.

The urge to walk into his arms and greet him with a good-morning kiss was strong. She had to remind herself that they weren't living together like husband and wife but as two people hiding from gunmen.

"Did you sleep okay last night?" It was an inane question to break the silence.

"Caught a few hours on the sofa." He broke two eggs in a bowl and whisked them with milk. "Pored over everything I could find online about Barton but still came up empty-handed."

She sipped her coffee, secretly doubting the clarity around Hawk's memory of seeing Barton in the Afghan mountains. The soldier in the photo was clearly not the senator, and she doubted that someone like Barton would be involved in selling American guns to the enemy.

"Mommy? I hav'ta go to the bathroom."

"Coming." Jillian put her coffee aside and went over to help her daughter get out of her footie pajamas. She took advantage of the opportunity to shower and to wash Lizzy up, too. When they were finished in the bathroom, Lizzy demanded to wear her Christmas outfit.

"Are you hungry?" Jillian tucked a strand of her wet hair behind her ear. "Mr. Hawk is making scrambled eggs for breakfast."

"Yum." Lizzy skipped as they entered the kitchen. "Did you add cheese?"

Hawk looked crestfallen at the plain eggs. "I'm sorry, but we don't have any cheese."

"That's okay. Lizzy likes scrambled eggs even without cheese," Jillian quickly interjected.

"Cheese makes them taste better," Lizzy pointed out.

"Next time." Hawk set the plate of scrambled eggs in front of their daughter and then a second plate with two eggs over easy in front of her.

Jillian waited until he joined them with his own eggs, also over easy. She put out a hand, inviting him to take it, at the same time reaching for Lizzy's. "Shall we pray?"

Hawk hesitated, then nodded. His hand was warm around hers but she refused to let that distract her. "Dear Lord, we thank You for keeping us safe and for this food we are about to eat. Please guide us on Your chosen path, amen."

"Amen," Lizzy mimicked.

"Amen," Hawk added in his hoarse voice.

She was pleased he'd joined in the prayer and stared for a moment at their joined hands, before forcing herself to let him go. James used to attend church with her, but it seemed as if Hawk had forgotten that part of his life.

She hoped and prayed Hawk would find his way back to his faith.

"The guys will be here in a couple of hours," Hawk said, breaking the silence.

Jillian glanced through the windows at the overcast sky. "That's fine. I'm hoping Lizzy can use the playground before it rains or snows."

"The temperature is above freezing, so it shouldn't snow."

"It would be nice to have a white Christmas," she said. Then she realized that what she should be praying for was to be safe at home, with the bad guys behind bars by Christmas.

A seemingly impossible task.

"I wanna swing!" Lizzy had glommed onto the comment about the playground. "And go down the slide!"

"We'll check it out after breakfast," Jillian promised.

"I'll tag along," Hawk said.

She was surprised by his offer. "I'm sure we're safe here if you have other things to do."

Hawk rubbed at his sore shoulder for a moment. "I don't have anything else to do until the guys get here."

"You've been taking your antibiotic, right?" she asked, noticing the gesture. "Maybe I should take a look at your wounds."

"The wounds are fine. The antibiotics are working, and the skin around the wound is red but not obviously infected. At least, not yet."

She feared it was only a matter of time but said nothing. Hawk would keep pressing forward until he was physically incapable of doing anything more. Wasn't that how he'd gotten himself out of the Appalachian Mountains? She could only imagine how difficult it had been for him to drag himself from the plane wreck, hiding while men combed the area for him, and then still managing to find relative safety.

It was humbling to realize the man she'd married had an underlying will of steel.

Upon finishing breakfast, Jillian began cleaning up and washing the dishes. Hawk joined her at the sink, pitching in to help.

"I can do this," she offered.

"I know. So can I."

She smiled and shook her head at his stubbornness. With the two of them working together, the task didn't take long, and soon they were bundled up in their outdoor gear and crossing the clearing toward the playground.

"I want Mr. Hawk to push me," Lizzy said after Jillian lifted her into the swing. "I wanna go really high!"

Hawk looked pleased with the request and eagerly stepped forward. Jillian moved back to give them room.

Hawk was tentative at first, pushing Lizzy carefully as if she were a fragile doll that might break. But Lizzy pumped her legs and cried, "Higher! I wanna go higher!"

He glanced at Jillian as if needing approval, before pushing Lizzy high in the air. The little girl squealed with glee and a wide smile softened Hawk's face.

"You should have figured she's a thrill seeker like her father," Jillian pointed out.

"Thrill seeker? I was never like that," he protested.

She arched a brow. "Have you forgotten that death trap of a motorcycle you used to ride before we got married?"

"Motorcycle? I drove a motorcycle?" He looked genuinely confused and she realized he hadn't remembered that part of their life. Those carefree days before he was sent overseas.

"Never mind." She waved a hand, wishing she'd never brought it up. "It doesn't matter."

When Lizzy got bored with the playground they headed back inside. She'd just found another movie on the kids' channel for Lizzy to watch when two SUVs pulled up in front of the cabin.

She recognized Mike Callahan, Matt Callahan and his K-9 Duchess, but the other man who emerged from the second SUV was a stranger.

Hawk opened the door and gestured for them to come inside.

"Hawk, you remember Ryker Tillman," Mike said, gesturing to the dark-haired stranger who wore his hair military short.

"Glad you could make it." Hawk held out his hand.

"You don't remember me, do you?" Ryker asked. "From years ago, not just the couple of months ago when we worked together to help Mike."

Hawk narrowed his gaze, staring at the guy intently. "You were in my special ops platoon. But not on my team."

Ryker smiled. "Is that a memory or a calculated guess?"

Hawk grimaced. "The latter, I'm afraid. My memory is still in bits and pieces."

"It's okay," Ryker assured him. "It was a long time ago. I'm just glad you're alive and well."

"Thanks. Oh, and this is Jillian."

"Ma'am," Ryker said with a nod.

"Please call me Jillian." She felt out of place amongst the group, so she went to the sink to boil some eggs, thinking it might be a good idea to have egg salad sandwiches for lunch. Not that there was enough food to feed all of them, but it gave her something to do.

"Ryker, I—um, need you to check out this photo for me." Hawk went over to pull the two photographs out of the brown envelope.

"Yeah, Mike texted a picture of them to me, but the image was too grainy to make out the guy's features." Ryker took the photographs from Hawk's hands and peered down at them for a long moment.

Jillian put the eggs in a pan of water and set them on the stove. After turning the electric burner on, she searched for the pan cover.

"I'm pretty sure this is Master Sergeant Colin Yonkers," Ryker said finally.

The pan cover slipped from Jillian's fingers, hitting the floor with a loud clang. The four men in the kitchen turned to stare at her in surprise.

"What's wrong?" Hawk sensed her distress. "Do you recognize the name?"

Jillian's mouth went dry and she reached a shaky hand toward the photograph. "I need to see that."

Ryker handed it over and she peered at the face of the American soldier standing next to the insurgent, who was holding some sort of assault rifle.

There was no mistake.

"It's him," she whispered. How could she have missed it the first time she'd looked at the photo?

"Who?" Hawk slipped his arm around her waist as if sensing she might fall.

She raised her gaze to his. "The man who came to tell me you were dead. Master Sergeant Colin Yonkers. I'm pretty sure I still have his card in the box of your things I kept in the basement."

Mike let out a low whistle. "That's an interesting twist."

Jillian stared at the photograph, double-checking to make sure it wasn't her own mind playing tricks on her.

But that day was clearly etched in her memory. This soldier in the photograph was the same man who'd come to tell her James had died in the line of duty.

But it was all a lie.

This man was the criminal responsible for the plane crash that had nearly killed Hawk.

The man who had taken away her husband.

NINE

Hawk tightened his grip around Jillian's waist. Her face was pale and her fingers trembled with fear or anger or both.

He could relate.

"Easy," he cautioned. His concern for Jillian momentarily displaced his anger over knowing that Yonkers had betrayed their country. Betrayed Hawk's team.

Had Yonkers been one of the soldiers who'd combed the wooded Appalachian mountainside for him? Hawk wished he could remember.

"I can't believe it," Jillian whispered. "The same man who sold guns to the enemy came to tell me you were dead."

"I know." He ached to pull her close and to kiss her but didn't want to make her uncomfortable in front of their audience.

"I remember Yonkers," Ryker spoke up.

Hawk turned to look at his fellow soldier. The one he hadn't remembered serving in Afghanistan with him. "What do you remember?"

Ryker hesitated a moment, glancing at Mike and Matt before continuing. "I remember he was trained as a special ops soldier, the way you and I were. I was assigned to the Charlie team, but you were in the Bravo team."

Bravo sounded right, although Hawk wished he could remember the names and faces of his teammates, the ones who had died in the plane crash, more clearly. "And where was Yonkers assigned?"

"Alpha team." Ryker shrugged and spread his hands. "We were all sent in different directions, to infiltrate the insurgents."

Hawk remembered that much, as well. "So the entire Alpha team could have been involved in the arms dealing. Who was their commanding officer?"

Again, Ryker looked puzzled. "All special ops teams reported up to the same commanding officer, Colonel McCann, now known as General McCann."

The name triggered something in Hawk's fragmented memory. "Major Rick Barton reported to the colonel, didn't he?"

Jillian sucked in a harsh breath.

"Yes, along with Major Todd Hayes," Ryker admitted. "But there were others, as well. It wasn't as if Yonkers was the captain in charge of Alpha, the way you were in charge of Bravo."

He'd been in charge of the Bravo team? Hawk hadn't remembered that, either. Maybe his mind had shut out all things military while he was in survival mode on the mountain. Memories that were too painful to deal with.

Or maybe he simply didn't remember as much as he'd originally thought. The memory fragment of Rick Barton could be nothing more than his imagination.

A cold tightness squeezed his chest. Did he have this all wrong? He'd been so focused on Barton—had he been chasing the wrong man?

None of it made any sense.

"We'll investigate Yonkers, see if we can find out what he's been up to these past five years," Mike said.

Hawk nodded. "He must have friends in high places to send highly trained men with guns after us."

"Understood," Mike agreed.

"Could be he's part of a mercenary group," Ryker offered. "A lot of soldiers joined them after leaving the army."

Mercenaries were known to take dangerous jobs for high pay. It was a possibility he hadn't considered. "You're right. It's an angle we need to explore."

Jillian pulled away from Hawk, quickly rinsed the pan cover she'd dropped and placed it over the eggs on the stove.

Hawk wished he knew what she was thinking.

Mike, Matt and Ryker took seats at the kitchen table. Hawk glanced at Jillian before joining them. She stood with her back to them, staring down at the pot of eggs, waiting for them to boil.

Mike took over the computer, using it with an ease Hawk envied. He could do the basics required to run his private investigator business but knew he lacked the skills Mike possessed. Pursuing a job as a private investigator allowed him the flexibility he needed to dig into Barton's past. With a faked background, he knew he'd never have made it into the police academy, and becoming a PI was the next best thing.

The pages on the screen flipped from one subject to the next as Mike started with some of the well-known mercenary groups.

"Here!" Excitement punctuated Mike's tone. He

turned the screen so Hawk could see it better. "Check this out."

"The Blake-Moore group?" Hawk shrugged. "I've never heard of them."

"Maybe not, but Yonkers's name is listed as a member. And look, the two founders are Kevin Blake and Harper Moore. They were soldiers, too. Does either of them look familiar to you?" Mike asked.

Hawk stared at the two photographs on the screen, trying to fit them into the empty puzzle-piece slots of his memory. "I don't think so. But Ryker would know better than I would."

Ryker slowly shook his head. "Sorry, but I can't place them, either. Could be they were over there, but I don't recognize them."

"It's a good find," Mike insisted. "I think it's possible the men who came after you and Jillian were members of this mercenary group."

"Because I have the photograph that implicates Yonkers?" Hawk tried to understand how this fitted. "Seems extreme. Why would Blake-Moore risk it? I ended up killing one of their men fighting back in self-defense."

"Maybe Blake or Moore were in on the arms deal?" Matt suggested. "If that was the case, they all have a lot to lose."

Hawk warmed to the idea. He wished he could place these two men who'd formed their own mercenary group. He tapped the screen. "Who hires these mercenary groups?"

Ryker, Matt and Mike all exchanged a knowing look.

"Anyone can hire them," Ryker finally said. "Private companies, for example, might need to hire protection for bigwigs traveling to dangerous areas of the continent."

"What about the US government?" Hawk pressed.

There was another moment of silence before Ryker nodded. "Yeah, I've heard that the government hires private groups like this, too. It's sometimes easier to use hired guns than to justify sending military troops."

That made sense to Hawk. "So guys like Barton and Hayes could have hired Yonkers and others to come after me."

"Anything is possible," Mike admitted. "But I'm not sure it's the likely scenario. Private groups like Blake-Moore don't have the same government oversight that the military has. Could be that Yonkers and whoever was working with him started something while deployed in Afghanistan and carried it over to the private sector."

"Yeah," Ryker chimed in. He spread his hands. "After all, who would know?"

"The weapons have to come from somewhere," Hawk pointed out.

"True. Maybe they still have an inside source within the army." Matt reached down to pat Duchess, who'd come in from the living room. "Regardless, it's a place to start."

The task of investigating a private mercenary group was daunting. Hawk had no idea where to start.

"I still have the letters you sent me," Jillian said, breaking the silence.

Hawk glanced at her with a frown. "Letters?"

"Yes." She turned to face him. "The ones you sent from Afghanistan. I'm certain you mentioned some of the guys by name."

For a moment he felt a surge of excitement and then remembered the damage done in her classroom. "I'm sure they already searched your house, Jilly," he gently pointed out. "The same way they searched your classroom."

"Yes, but they missed the envelope in my classroom. Maybe they missed the letters, as well?" Jillian had taken the eggs off the stove and was running them under cold water. "When I was going through your things, I took the letters and put them in Lizzy's room. They may not have found them there."

Hawk considered the possibility. As much as he wanted to know what was in the letters he'd sent his wife, he wasn't convinced they would be helpful. "Not sure it's worth the risk. If I was Yonkers and had mercenaries to do my bidding, I'd have someone staked out at your place. The same way they were staked out at the school."

"Would be nice to know what information may be in the letters," Mike pointed out. "Who knows, maybe you mention either Kevin Blake or Harper Moore by name."

"It would be a good link to have," Ryker agreed. "Something to go along with the photographs."

"I can show you where the letters are," Jillian offered.

"No. You're not going along this time," Hawk said firmly. "Remember last time?"

Jillian stared at him for a long moment. He tried not to fidget in his seat. It was almost impossible for him to deny Jillian anything, but he knew forcing her to stay safe with Lizzy was the right thing to do.

She broke away from his gaze and left the kitchen without saying a word.

Taking a big chunk of his heart with her.

Jillian plopped on the sofa next to Lizzy, fighting the urge to cry.

She wasn't sure why she was so upset. After experiencing the gunfire at the school, she'd decided her role was to stay with Lizzy, to keep her safe.

But she wanted Hawk to be safe, too.

The thought of losing him made her sick to her stomach.

She couldn't lose him. Not after finding him after all these years.

"Mommy, will you play dolls with me?" Lizzy asked.

She forced a smile. "Sure."

Lizzy took a throw blanket from the sofa and made a tent over the coffee table. "This will be Belle's house."

"I see," Jillian commented. Her daughter was creative when it came to playing, and Jillian remembered how she and James had once talked about having a large family.

At the time, she hadn't wanted Lizzy to be an only child like her. James had agreed.

Did Hawk even remember that conversation? She doubted it.

Jillian closed her eyes for a moment, reaching out in prayer. God would watch over them.

Hadn't He watched over James during the past five years?

The murmur of male voices piqued her interest, but she forced herself to play with Lizzy. Caring for her daughter was the most important thing right now.

She never should have mentioned the letters.

Lizzy played with Belle, making the doll dance under the tent as if the area were a ballroom. Jillian used a stubby stick from the wood sitting in front of the fireplace and used it as the Beast.

When Hawk had chosen Belle as a gift for Lizzy, had he envisioned himself as the Beast? She hoped not. The scar didn't matter, it was the man inside that was attractive to her.

They played for a while before Hawk interrupted

them. "Jilly? The guys are going to head out to get sandwiches for lunch. What would you and Lizzy like?"

"I was going to make egg salad sandwiches for the group," she protested.

"No! I want a grilled cheese," Lizzy announced.

"We can save the eggs for breakfast. Is that okay with you, Jillian?" Hawk asked.

She shrugged. "Sure, why not?"

"What would you like to eat?"

"Turkey with cheese, lettuce and tomato," she responded. "When are you leaving?"

"Not until later this evening. Maybe nine or ten tonight."

She nodded, understanding the need to go in while it was dark.

Hawk went back into the kitchen to relay their order but then returned shortly thereafter. "Will you please tell me exactly where you put the letters?"

She didn't answer right away, listening as Lizzy sang the opening song to *Beauty and the Beast*. "In Lizzy's closet," she finally told him. "There's a small lace-covered jewelry box that I found at a secondhand store. There's a velvet shelf inside that lifts out. The area underneath is meant for larger jewelry but I used that as a place to store the letters."

"Is that where you put your diamond engagement ring?" he asked.

"Yes." She lifted her gaze to his. "There's also one of our wedding photos in there. Those were the keepsakes I was saving for Lizzy."

"Thank you." Hawk tucked a strand of her hair behind her ear. "I appreciate that you tried to keep me in our daughter's heart."

Suddenly it was all too much. "Don't go. Stay here with us. I'm sure the others can find the letters without your help."

The words had barely left her mouth when Hawk shook his head. "I can't do that. This is my problem. It's bad enough I'm exposing my friends to danger. I need to be the one to take the biggest risk."

He was right. Logically, she understood, but her heart rejected everything about Hawk being in the center of danger.

"How's your shoulder?"

"Fine." His gaze skidded from hers in a way that convinced her he was stretching the truth.

"I want to see it." This time, she wasn't taking no for an answer. If the wounds were dramatically worse, then she'd insist he allow one of the others to go inside Lizzy's room to get the letters.

Hawk let out a sigh and nodded. "Fine. But I'm telling you it looks okay. At least the front does. It's hard to see the entry wound in the back."

"I'll be the judge of that." She gestured for him to sit at the other end of the sofa.

He slipped his arm out of the T-shirt and showed her his shoulder. The dressings covering the front and the back looked fresh from the morning. She peeked beneath the gauze, not liking the redness that puckered the edges of his skin. To her eyes, the front wound looked worse than the back.

"I'm not sure how much longer you can let this go with just oral antibiotics." She set the old dressings aside and left to get fresh gauze. The packets were in the bathroom and she returned and quickly redressed them.

Dear Reader,

Since you are a lover of our books, your opinions are important to us... and so is your time.

That's why we made sure your **"FAST FIVE" READER SURVEY** can be completed in just a few minutes. Your answers to the five questions will help us remain at the forefront of women's fiction.

And, as a thank-you for participating, we'd like to send you up to **4 FREE BOOKS** and **FREE THANK-YOU GIFTS!**

Try **Love Inspired® Romance Larger-Print** books featuring Christian characters facing modern-day challenges.

Try **Love Inspired® Suspense Larger-Print** novels featuring Christian characters facing challenges to their faith... and lives.

Or TRY BOTH!

Enjoy your gifts with our appreciation,

Pam Powers

To get up to
4 FREE BOOKS & THANK-YOU GIFTS:

✳ Quickly complete the "Fast Five" Reader Survey
and return the insert.

"FAST FIVE" READER SURVEY

1 Do you sometimes read a book a second or third time? ○ Yes ○ No

2 Do you often choose reading over other forms of entertainment such as television? ○ Yes ○ No

3 When you were a child, did someone regularly read aloud to you? ○ Yes ○ No

4 Do you sometimes take a book with you when you travel outside the home? ○ Yes ○ No

5 In addition to books, do you regularly read newspapers and magazines? ○ Yes ○ No

YES! Please send me my Free Rewards, consisting of **2 Free Books from each series I select** and **Free Mystery Gifts**. I understand that I am under no obligation to buy anything, as explained on the back of this card.

❏ **Love Inspired® Romance Larger-Print** (122/322 IDL GNSN)
❏ **Love Inspired® Suspense Larger-Print** (107/307 IDL GNSN)
❏ **Try Both** (122/322 & 107/307 IDL GNSY)

FIRST NAME	LAST NAME

ADDRESS

APT.#	CITY

STATE/PROV.	ZIP/POSTAL CODE

LI/SLI-819-FF19

"They're working fine." Hawk winced as he put his arm through his shirtsleeve. "I've suffered worse."

She knew he meant after the plane crash. The strength of will he'd used to survive in the mountains amazed her. She wanted to throw herself into his arms, but the low rumble of a car engine indicated the guys were back with the promised food.

The rest of the day passed by with excruciating slowness. Lizzy was pretty good at keeping herself occupied, but by the time they were finished with dinner, even her daughter's mood had turned cranky.

"Bath time," Jillian announced, eager to get her daughter down for the night.

"Okay!" Lizzy happened to like baths and eagerly ran toward the bathroom.

"Jilly." Hawk caught her hand before she could follow their daughter. "We're heading out. Keep your disposable phone handy, okay? Matt and Duchess are going to stay here with you while the rest of us head into town."

"I know." She was glad to have Duchess around, since the dog kept Lizzy entertained. "Hawk, promise me you'll be careful."

His blue eyes bored into hers. "I promise."

She gave him a quick hug and a kiss, then pulled away to follow Lizzy, feeling the intensity of Hawk's gaze on her back as she went.

The only thing she could do now was to wait. And pray.

Dear Lord, keep Hawk and the others safe in Your care!

Hawk hated leaving Jilly and Lizzy at the cabin but reminded himself they would be safe with Matt and Duchess watching over them.

He desperately needed some sort of break in the case. Having the photo of Yonkers with the insurgent was a start, but he needed more.

It was a lot of hope to pin on a handful of old love letters.

The trip to Brookland seemed to take longer than it had the previous day. Hawk didn't want to believe it was because Jillian and Lizzy weren't with him, but he couldn't deny the keen sense of loss.

How had he become so dependent on them? For the past five months he'd been content to live nearby, offering nothing more than a helping hand.

Now he wanted more. Maybe even a chance at a future.

An impossible dream if he couldn't figure out who was behind the recent attacks.

"I think I need to pay Yonkers a visit," Ryker said, breaking the silence. "Maybe I can infiltrate the Blake-Moore organization."

"Not yet," Hawk protested. He didn't like the idea of any of his friends being in danger. "We don't even know if they're involved. This could be something Yonkers did on his own."

"Then maybe we should kidnap him and bring him to the cabin for questioning," Ryker pointed out. "It's a way to get to the heart of the issue. Your wife and daughter deserve to be safe."

Hawk was touched by Ryker's offer but wasn't convinced. "Hold that thought for now. We'll go that route if we have to."

"The address you gave me is on the next block," Mike said from the driver's seat. "Where do you want me to park?"

"Here is fine." Hawk zipped up his leather jacket and

pulled on his gloves. Jilly's keys were in his pocket, but he suspected he'd find the door already open, the way the school's had been.

"We'll give you ten minutes," Ryker said. "If you're not back by then, we're coming in after you."

"Got it." Hawk silently acknowledged he'd missed working with a team. Being with Ryker and the Callahans reminded him of the men he'd served with on the Bravo team.

He straightened. Bravo team! He had a clear memory of standing outside their camp with the men of his team. He wished more memories would fall into place. The sooner the better.

Hawk slipped out of the car and into the darkness. The earlier sunshine had melted much of the snow, making it easy to avoid leaving tracks as he approached Jilly's.

As expected, the door was ajar. The interior had been ransacked the same way her classroom had been, only worse. The Christmas tree was on its side, the ornaments broken into dozens of pieces. He clenched his jaw, furious at how they'd ruined Jillian's home. Holding his temper in check, he carefully made his way to the upstairs bedrooms.

Lizzy's room had been searched but not messed up like the living room. Inside the closet, he found the lacy jewelry box. He checked to make sure the engagement ring and the letters were inside.

They were. With a sense of relief, Hawk tucked the box beneath his arm and moved back across the room.

A creak on the staircase on the other side of the door made him freeze in his tracks.

Someone was out there!

TEN

As much as he didn't want to let go of the jewelry box with the letters, Hawk carefully set it down on the floor so he would have both hands free. He didn't move for ten full minutes, waiting for the hostile on the stairs to reveal himself. He didn't so much as blink, keeping all five of his senses laser sharp. When he heard the slightest brush of fabric against the wall, he knew his patience had been rewarded.

Yet he continued to wait. When he heard another sound, closer this time, he mentally judged the distance between himself and the doorway to Lizzy's room.

Not yet, he warned himself, despite the fact that every muscle in his body was tense with the need to move.

Another sound and the barest movement of the door. *Now!*

Hawk lashed out with his booted foot, kicking the door into the intruder. There was a muffled thump, but then the door flew open, nearly hitting him in the face.

The intruder came straight for Hawk like a mini bulldozer. Hawk used the guy's momentum to spin him around, slamming him into the wall. Hawk's momentary satisfaction evaporated when the guy continued to fight, hitting and kicking with all his might, refusing to go down easy.

Hawk took several blows, including one directly in his injured shoulder, which caused a red haze of pain to cloud his vision. Gritting his teeth and ignoring the pain, he wrapped his fingers around the guy's neck, wrestling him to the floor. He continued to hold pressure against his carotid arteries, until the hostile's strength faded. When he felt the man's body go limp, he eased upright and took a moment to draw in a ragged breath.

His shoulder throbbed and he could feel the dampness of fresh blood oozing from the through-and-through bullet wounds. He sighed. Man, he was getting too old for this. He found some of Lizzy's hair ribbons and used them to bind the attacker's wrists, then took off the guy's boots so he could use the shoelaces to tie up his ankles. Once he had the intruder trussed up like a Christmas turkey, Hawk pulled off the ski mask and waited for him to regain consciousness.

This ridiculous game of hide-and-seek had gone on long enough. He wanted answers.

And this time, he wasn't leaving until he had them.

Knowing Mike and Ryker would be waiting, Hawk called Mike's phone. "I've got a hostile tied up here, will be out soon."

"Did you find the letters?" Mike asked.

"Yes." Hawk disconnected the call because the guy on the floor began to move. When the hostile realized he was tied up, he stopped his struggles and looked up at Hawk.

"Who sent you?"

The assailant didn't answer. Hawk felt his body tense with frustration. He leaned over, getting in the guy's face.

"Who sent you?" he repeated, his low, gravelly voice harsh with anger.

Again, the man didn't respond.

Hawk pulled out his gun and put the barrel against the perp's temple. "Give me one good reason not to kill you right here, right now."

There was another pause, but the frightened look in the guy's widened eyes gave Hawk hope that he'd start talking.

"I'm following orders," the intruder finally said.

"Whose orders?" Hawk pressed the barrel of the gun more firmly against his temple. "Who from the Blake-Moore group is giving the orders?"

The surprise in the guy's eyes confirmed Hawk was on the right track. "If I talk they'll kill me."

"I'll kill you if you don't." Hawk hoped and prayed the guy wouldn't call his bluff. "Which one? Kevin Blake or Harper Moore?"

"Moore," the man finally admitted.

The answer surprised him. "Why?"

The intruder shook his head. "I don't know. I just do what I'm told."

"Tell me your name. And if you were you one of the men up at the cabin." Hawk pressed.

The guy's gaze skittered from his in a way that confirmed Hawk's suspicions.

"I guess I should have killed you then." Hawk stared down at the guy. "Why did you go after Jillian Wade?"

"We weren't supposed to hurt her. We only wanted the photographs."

Hawk nodded. So far this guy was confirming their suspicions, but he needed more. "Who hired the Blake-Moore group to come after me?"

The intruder shook his head. "I don't know. I told you, my job is to follow orders."

"What's your name?" Hawk wasn't sure why he cared so much about who this guy was, but he wanted to verify he was former army, too. He didn't think a private mercenary group would hire anyone but former military, but maybe former law enforcement?

"Ben Dugan."

"Okay, Dugan. Tell me about the weapons being sold in Afghanistan."

Dugan frowned. "I don't know anything about that."

Hawk wasn't sure he believed him. A noise at the doorway had him spinning around with his weapon ready. But it was only Tillman who'd come to offer assistance.

Hawk turned back to his hostage. "You said you only wanted the photographs. You didn't know what was on them?"

"No. I don't have any idea what you're talking about."

"We can make him talk," Ryker drawled.

"I'm not sure he knows anything," Hawk answered.

There was a long silence as Hawk considered his options. It wouldn't necessarily surprise him that the boss of the operation had withheld key information from his men. Yet he knew Dugan had every reason to lie.

"Fine. Don't tell me about the gun sales. We'll figure out the rest on our own." Hawk glanced at Ryker, who shrugged and nodded.

"What should we do with him?" Ryker asked.

Hawk gestured toward the door. "We'll leave, then call the police. They can arrest him for trespassing and vandalism."

"No! Wait! Don't! They'll kill me!"

After tucking the frilly jewelry box beneath his arm, Hawk hesitated, staring down at the mercenary. "And if I don't turn you in to the authorities, you'll just come after me again. I can't risk it."

"I have money saved up, they pay us well." Dugan's tone was pleading. "Let me go and I'll disappear."

He wasn't sure he believed him, but at the same time, he didn't want any more blood on his hands. The one mercenary he'd killed in self-defense was more than enough.

"I'll take care of him for you," Ryker offered. "I'll haul his butt into town and dump him on the cops' doorstep."

Hawk appreciated it but shook his head. "It's not worth it."

"We can't just leave him here," Ryker pointed out.

"Sure we can. We'll give him fifteen minutes before calling the cops. That seems fair enough." Hawk headed toward Ryker, then glanced over his shoulder. "And Dugan?" Hawk waited until the guy looked him in the eye. "If I see you again, I will kill you."

Dugan didn't answer, but Hawk didn't care. Getting out of his binds wouldn't be easy, but it was possible. Hawk followed Ryker as they stealthily made their way through Jilly's house and out the back door, making sure to take care in case Dugan hadn't been alone.

But they didn't see anyone else when they met up with Mike at the SUV.

Ryker jumped into the back, leaving Hawk to ride shotgun. He settled into the seat and glanced at his friend. "In twelve minutes, we're going to call the police and report the intruder and subsequent vandalism," Hawk told him.

Mike lifted a brow at the strange request but didn't ask anything further. "What did you find out?"

"His name is Ben Dugan and he works for the Blake-Moore group, as we suspected. He claims his orders came directly from Harper Moore and that the intent was only to get the photographs from Jillian without hurting her or Lizzy."

Mike let out a snort. "Yeah, right."

Hawk gingerly rotated his injured shoulder, understanding where Mike was coming from. The bullet hadn't been a warning but an attempt to silence him for good. And it galled him to know that his body had protected Jillian and Lizzy. If the bullet had been lower... he shook his head, unable to finish the thought.

"You and Ryker left him tied up?" Mike asked, breaking the silence.

"Yeah. Gave him fifteen minutes to get away before calling the cops."

"Why?" Mike asked, his expression mirroring his confusion. "Don't you want him arrested?"

"I do but he claims the mercenaries will kill him if he gets caught by the cops. Figured we'd give him a chance to escape."

Mike glanced at the rearview mirror, exchanging a look with Ryker. Hawk knew they were curious about his motives, but he didn't care. Hawk closed his eyes, trying to relax despite feeling every blow Dugan had landed.

The wound in his shoulder would need medical attention, soon. Hawk fought off the sense of overwhelming despair. He'd gotten the letters and a small amount of information, but still nothing solid to go on.

He needed to find a way to keep Jillian and Lizzy safe from the mercenaries who stalked him. No easy task, considering the wealth and power these men had to get what they wanted.

Remembering how Jillian had prayed made him wonder if that would help. Was God really up there, looking out for him? He felt as if it was worth a try.

He sent up a silent prayer, asking for the strength and wisdom to keep his wife and daughter safe from harm.

Relishing the sense of peace that washed over him.

Jillian couldn't relax while Hawk, Mike and Ryker were gone. Oh, she appreciated Matt's being here with Duchess to watch over them, but it wasn't the same as having Hawk protect her and Lizzy.

Strange how much she'd come to lean on Hawk over these past few days. To the point she didn't feel safe or at ease without him at her side.

Matt's phone rang. Jillian leaped up from the sofa, her stomach knotting with worry. She trusted in Hawk's abilities and was grateful he wasn't alone, but she feared the call was bad news.

"Yeah, I'm looking him up now," Matt said as he tapped the computer keyboard.

Jillian came up to stand beside him, anxious to know what was going on.

"I found Benjamin Dugan, and he's former army and was stationed in Afghanistan the same time you were."

"Is Hawk okay?" she whispered.

Matt nodded, then put his hand over the phone. "Yeah, they're all on their way back. This is Ryker on the phone. They were able to get a name from one of the mercenaries."

Relieved to know Hawk was okay, Jillian sank into the kitchen chair beside Matt and kept her gaze on the army soldier on the screen.

"He was Team Alpha, too," Matt continued. He put the phone on speaker so he could work as he talked. "I have a photo here of him with Yonkers. Guess that explains why he joined the Blake-Moore group."

"We need to know who gave the Alpha team their orders," Ryker said. "I think it's clear that the Alpha team has turned mercenary. But we need a connection to someone higher up on the food chain."

"Agreed." Matt continued searching the images, moving so fast on the screen she couldn't keep up. "I'll dig around a bit more. Just get here as soon as you can."

"Did you find the letters?" Jillian asked before Ryker could end the call.

"Yeah, Hawk found them."

"Were any of the names in the letters familiar?" She wanted to believe the letters were useful, that this little excursion hadn't been for nothing.

"I can't answer that yet, it's too dark to read them. We'll take a closer look when we get there."

Jillian sensed there was something Ryker wasn't telling her but decided to let it go. Matt had told her Hawk was okay, so she did her best to be patient.

"No reason for you to wait up," Matt said, scratching Duchess behind the ears.

She gave him a blank stare. "I couldn't sleep even if I wanted to."

Matt sighed and nodded. Sitting there with nothing constructive to do was excruciating. She wanted to help with the investigation. Doing what, she had no clue.

She tried to remember the contents of Hawk's— James's—love letters, but couldn't remember anything other than how much he'd missed her.

And she'd missed him, too. Especially the morning when she'd found out she was pregnant. Then the fateful knock had come on her door just hours later, revealing a man wearing a full-dress blue uniform.

She'd known James was dead the moment she saw the man standing there. She'd been sick to her stomach, either from the devastating news or the effects of her pregnancy. Or both.

Except James hadn't been dead. He'd been in a plane crash and left for dead, surviving against all odds.

She was so lost in the memories, that she didn't hear the SUV drive up until she heard voices coming from outside. When Hawk stepped through the doorway, she lunged up from her seat and threw herself into his arms.

He caught her against his chest and held her close for several long moments. It wasn't until one of the guys loudly cleared his throat that she realized they were blocking the doorway.

"Sorry," she murmured, stepping back from Hawk's embrace. She frowned when she noticed fresh blood stains on his shirt. "You're hurt!"

"It's nothing." Hawk moved into the kitchen so that Ryker and Mike could come in out of the cold. "The wound opened up a bit, that's all."

She sent a steely glare toward Ryker, who couldn't look her in the eye. "You said he was fine."

"I am. Leave him alone, Jilly," Hawk said gently. "We got what we went for and more."

The jewelry box looked incongruous in Hawk's rough hands. He held it out toward her, but she shook her head.

"You should look at them. The names will mean more to you than to me."

Hawk nodded and carefully set the box on the table. He went over to wash his hands at the sink before returning to open the jewelry box. When Jillian saw her engagement ring, tears pricked her eyes.

She'd taken the diamond ring off on the one-year anniversary of James's death. So long ago, yet at the same time, it seemed like yesterday.

Hawk caught her gaze for a moment before lifting out the top part of the jewelry box to reveal the letters tucked beneath. He pulled them out and set them on the table.

The ribbon she'd used to tie them together was pink, old and frayed. She'd chosen the color for Lizzy. It was still her daughter's favorite color.

Hawk put the letters in order, the most recent on top, as she took the seat next to him. He carefully opened the last letter he'd ever written to her and began to read.

Seeing his tight, messy scrawl brought fond memories to the surface. She remembered how much she looked forward to hearing from James, hanging on every word he'd written. Reading them over and over until the paper grew worn and thin.

A burst of anger at what they'd lost, at what had been taken from them, sent her stumbling to her feet. She went into the living room and collapsed on the sofa, burying her face in her hands as she tried to hold herself together.

She knew she should be grateful for finding Hawk after all these years. To know he was alive and had found his way home to her.

But the acute sense of loss wouldn't go away. How different would her life and Lizzy's be if James hadn't seen something he shouldn't have?

Useless to play the what-if game.

"Jilly." Hawk's low voice caused her to lift her head from her hands. The cushion shifted as he sat beside her. "We're going to be all right. I promise to keep you safe."

He misunderstood what was behind her emotional breakdown. "I'm so angry at the men who did this to you," she finally managed. "To us."

"Anger won't help us figure out the person responsible for all of this," he pointed out in a reasonable tone that made her want to shove him off the sofa.

"Maybe not, but I can't help it. They tried to kill you. Took you away from me, from Lizzy. It's not right! They had no right to do that to us!"

"Easy." Hawk's tone was soothing as he put his arm around her shoulders. "We'll get to the bottom of this. The men responsible will go to jail for a very long time."

At the moment it wasn't much comfort. Leaning against Hawk, she tried to rein in her temper.

He was right. Getting angry wouldn't help them understand who was responsible.

She lifted her head and looked at him. "Did the letters help?"

There was a moment's hesitation before he nodded. "I mentioned Colin Yonkers several times. He was part of the Alpha team, and from what I can tell—we were once friends."

Friends? She stared into Hawk's blue eyes and saw the regret. This news, along with his concussion, could explain his repressed memories. She couldn't imagine finding out your friend was selling guns to the enemy.

And worse? Knowing the same friend tried to kill you to keep the secret from seeing the light of day.

ELEVEN

Hawk didn't want to tell Jillian how difficult it had been for him to read the letters he'd written to her so many years ago. Most of the time it was as if they were written by a stranger. More proof that he was a different man back then, as revealed by letters full of love, hope and faith. Until the day he'd lost his entire team in a plane crash, which had left a hard, cracked, scarred shell of a man behind.

His stomach knotted with the realization that the love he'd once shared with Jillian was gone forever. That simple, pure love was something they could never get back.

He told himself to focus on the fact that he was here with Jillian and Lizzy now. The way she leaned on him, and had gotten so upset with Yonkers on his behalf, was sweet.

The letters hadn't revealed as much as he'd hoped. Although, in addition to several mentions of Yonkers, there was also one brief reference to Major Rick Barton. The phrasing gave him the impression that the Bravo team had reported up through Barton.

Was that reporting relationship the reason he still had that snippet of memory about the guy? And if so, had Yonkers's Alpha team reported up to Barton as well?

What did it all mean?

"Hawk?" Jillian's soft voice drew him from his swirling thoughts.

"What is it?" He kept his arm around her shoulders, holding her close.

"I'm glad you're here with me. With us."

Her words were a soothing balm against the jagged edges of his heart. He ached to kiss her, but the guys were still in the kitchen, so he refrained from giving in to temptation.

"When this is over…" Jillian began, but he silenced her with a finger over her lips.

"Don't, Jilly." He couldn't help remembering those letters. The words of love James had written. "I don't want you to make any rash promises. We'll just take things one step at a time, okay? Ensuring your safety and Lizzy's is my one and only priority."

"Hawk…" she tried again, but he shook his head and gently pulled away from her.

"The man you once loved is gone, Jilly. Reading those letters proves it. I'm not that guy anymore. James is gone, forever. And no amount of hoping and praying will bring him back."

Jilly jumped to her feet, temper sparking in her green gaze. "Hawk and James are more alike than you realize. They share a brain and a heart. Don't you see? That's all that matters."

He sighed, knowing she was missing the point. But then she continued, "Of course you're different now. Any soldier who serves overseas in combat comes home a changed man. You know that as well as I do. I'm not the same woman I was when we first married, either. Being a mother changed me. Honestly, Hawk, if you would put your future in God's hands, you'd find out exactly what God has in store for us."

Her words resonated deep within. He remembered the faith he'd displayed in his letters. Was Jillian right about rediscovering his faith? Was that part of the heart and brain he shared with James? He remembered how his earlier prayer had brought a sense of peace.

"Okay, you're right," he finally said. "We've both changed, and focusing on the past isn't helpful. We'll move forward from here, together."

"I'd like that," Jillian agreed.

He held up a hand. "But keeping you and Lizzy safe is still the main priority."

"Your safety, too," Jillian added.

His gaze held hers for a long moment. It humbled him to know she cared about him.

About Hawk. The man he'd become.

"Hawk? You need to see this." Mike Callahan's voice interrupted his thoughts.

"Be right there." He wanted to reach out to Jillian but tucked his hands in the front pockets of his jeans. "Get some rest. I'm not sure how long the guys will stay, but you need sleep."

She hesitated before nodding. "Good night, Hawk."

"Good night."

He watched her enter the bedroom she shared with Lizzy. He felt as if the earth had shifted slightly to the left and he was having trouble regaining his footing. The idea that she saw parts of James within him was disconcerting.

"Hawk?" Mike repeated.

He returned to the kitchen to see what the guys had found.

"Check this out." Mike tapped a photo on the computer screen. "We did a search on Barton and found this."

A chill snaked down Hawk's spine. "Colin Yonkers."

"Yep. That's a picture of your old buddy Yonkers shaking hands and looking all chummy with Senator Rick Barton."

"When was that taken?"

"Two years ago," Ryker spoke up. "So far we haven't found anything more recent."

A handshake at some charity function from two years ago wasn't the link he was hoping to find, but it was a start.

"Listen, Hawk, I need to hit the road, I promised Lacy I'd be back tonight. She has her hands full with Rory and being pregnant." Matt Callahan stood near the door, with Duchess at his side. "I took some time off work. So I can return tomorrow, if that helps."

Hawk realized the hour was half past midnight. "Yeah, sure. Why don't all of you get out of here? You have families to take care of."

"I don't," Ryker said dryly. "Maybe we should call Duncan O'Hare—he doesn't have a family, either."

Hawk reluctantly grinned. Once he'd felt just like Tillman and O'Hare, alone in a world where Callahans were falling in love like apples dropping from trees. "No sense in dragging Duncan into this. And you still have a life, don't you?"

Ryker shrugged. "Not really. Been feeling at loose ends."

"You're welcome to bunk here. There's a third bedroom no one is using. But don't feel obligated to stick around. You can always return in the morning with the others."

Ryker shrugged. "No sense in driving back and forth. After being in Afghanistan, I've learned to sleep anywhere."

Hawk was touched by the offer and wondered if Ryker was doing this because of his own experiences in Afghanistan. Ryker had mentioned being on Team Charlie, and Hawk was curious about what Ryker had gone through back then.

Not that Ryker's secrets were any of his business.

"Not sure what more we can do until the morning anyway," Mike said, rising to his feet and stretching his cramped muscles. "Even if we find more photos of Yonkers and Senator Barton together, it won't mean anything. We need to talk directly with Yonkers."

"Or with someone else from Alpha," Ryker added. "Dugan didn't know anything, but someone else will. Yonkers didn't pull this off on his own. I'll see if I can find anyone that might be in the area."

"Thanks again," Hawk said as the Callahans made their way outside.

"We've got your back," Mike said, clapping him on his uninjured shoulder. "The same way you had ours."

Hawk nodded. He hadn't thought twice about helping Mike and the other Callahan siblings when they'd run into trouble over the past couple of years. It had honestly never occurred to him that he'd one day need their help in return.

Yet here he was, needing everything they had to offer and grateful for it. Nothing was more important than keeping Jillian and Lizzy safe.

When their taillights faded out of sight, he went back inside. Ryker had taken the seat behind the computer. Hawk rubbed his throbbing shoulder—he knew he couldn't put off cleaning the wound any longer. So far, the antibiotics Dana had obtained for him were keeping the infection at bay. But he was feeling chilled and hoped he wasn't running a fever.

"You should get some rest," Ryker said as if reading his thoughts. "I'll work here for a bit longer and then hit the sack."

"Okay, thanks." Hawk wasn't about to argue. He headed into the bathroom and shucked out of his T-shirt. Fresh blood oozed from the saturated gauze over the wound. Gritting his teeth, he removed the old dressing and then used soap and water to clean the wound as best he could.

Unfortunately, he couldn't reach the entry wound in the back of his shoulder very easily. He slapped water over his shoulder, making a mess. The exit wound in the front was worse, but he knew that either one of them could be a source of infection. The ibuprofen would help, but not for long.

They needed to find a way to get to the bottom of this mess. Before he ended up in the hospital.

Reminding himself to drink more fluids, Hawk finished redressing his wounds and returned to the kitchen to chug down a full glass of water with the ibuprofen.

Antibiotics, fluids, ibuprofen and rest. That was all he could do for the moment.

But when he stretched out on his bed, his mind wouldn't shut down. He kept thinking about the letters he'd written to Jillian so many years ago.

She'd told him that Hawk and James were entwined together, and maybe she was right. His basic personality couldn't have changed that much.

But when he read those letters, he'd felt as if he were

eavesdropping on a conversation between Jillian and someone else. A relationship that made him jealous.

He knew that his experience in the Appalachian Mountains had changed him. Jillian could say that a part of James was still with him, but how did she know for sure? Especially when he couldn't be certain?

The thought scared him. Far more than four hostiles coming after him.

Because he knew that if he gave his heart to Jillian and she decided that she didn't love Hawk the way she once had loved James, he would never recover.

He couldn't lose Jillian twice in one lifetime. That was too much to ask of any man.

Which meant he needed to keep a bit of distance between them, until she honestly accepted him for who he was.

Hawk Jacobson, not James Wade.

Jillian woke early in the morning. The darkness lingering beyond the windows proved that dawn hadn't yet broken over the horizon. The air was chilly, but aside from that, the atmosphere was so nice and peaceful she decided to stay snuggled under the covers. There was no reason to be up this soon. Besides, she wasn't sure how many of the guys had stayed overnight in the cabin. It would perhaps be better to wait before finding out.

And she really didn't want to wake Lizzy up yet. Her daughter had dealt with all of this running for safety like a champ, but Jillian had no idea how much longer Lizzy would tolerate being in the cabin without her friends at day care or any of her things to play with.

Her thoughts circled around to last night's conversation with Hawk. Deep down, she was troubled by the way he felt so completely severed from James. It just didn't make any sense. She believed that, at the core, Hawk and James were the same man.

Granted, a terrible tragedy could change a person's outlook on life, altering how they saw the world, but it couldn't change who you were deep within.

Or could it?

She didn't want to entertain the notion that he might be right. Not after how Hawk had acted around her since the night he'd caught those men sneaking into her home. She'd witnessed Hawk's actions firsthand over these past few days and knew that he hadn't changed much from the man she'd fallen in love with. A little, sure. But not a lot.

After all, she'd changed, too. Hawk didn't seem to appreciate the ways she was different. Was that because he didn't remember their lives before his deployment as clearly as she did?

Those days were gone, but that didn't mean they couldn't experience them again in the future. Even if they decided to give their relationship a try, especially since Hawk deserved to be in close contact with Lizzy, she wasn't sure that he'd understand her need to maintain her financial independence. She was on Christmas break now but planned to be back in her classroom at Brookland Elementary when school resumed after the New Year.

James had told her he preferred her to stay home once they had a family. He'd been a latchkey kid and hadn't liked it, so he'd wanted something different, something better, for his own children.

Yet upon learning of James's death, she'd faced the cold, hard reality that she needed to be able to support herself and Lizzy. Thankfully, she'd finished her teaching degree and was able to find a job, but it hadn't been easy.

Now that Hawk was back in her life, she understood he may be able to provide for her and Lizzy financially, but she wasn't about to give up her hard-earned independence.

Nope. Giving up her teaching job wasn't going to work for her. She liked spending time with her students. They certainly kept her on her toes. Even more important, she enjoyed her admittedly minor role in shaping their future. Any one of these children she taught had a chance to do something amazing with their lives.

Especially Lizzy.

She thought about what to make for breakfast and wished she hadn't made the hard-boiled eggs yesterday. She didn't mind having them for breakfast, but Lizzy wasn't a fan. There might be pancake batter, which would work, but she couldn't remember if there was any syrup.

Realizing she couldn't stay here any longer, she slid out of bed and padded across the room, hoping not to wake Lizzy.

When she opened the door she was surprised to find Hawk and Ryker seated at the kitchen table. The scent of coffee was welcome, so she slid through the doorway, softly closing the door behind her.

After quickly using the bathroom, Jillian entered the kitchen and helped herself to a mug of coffee.

"Good morning." Hawk's greeting was sweet. The man she'd met a few days ago had never indulged in small talk.

"Morning," she returned, adding milk to her mug. "What's going on?"

The two men exchanged a glance that made her put

her mug down on the counter. Something was obviously up and she sensed she wouldn't like it.

"We found Yonkers," Hawk finally admitted. "And we're thinking of going after him."

Yup, she didn't like it. Not one bit. "Why? Isn't this a job for the police? Can't you call in the authorities and make them take care of him?"

"Based on what proof?" Ryker asked reasonably. "A grainy five-year-old photo? It's not enough."

She opened her mouth to argue, but Hawk held up his hand. "Jilly, hold off a minute. We just want to talk to Colin Yonkers, nothing more."

"He has a sister in the area," Ryker continued. "We're going to head over there as soon as the Callahans return."

She still didn't like it. "His sister is innocent. Why drag her into this?"

"So are you and Lizzy," Hawk countered. "And again, we're not going to hurt her or drag her into anything. We just need to talk to her brother."

She crossed her arms over her chest, feeling helpless. She didn't want to be left with one of the Callahans as a babysitter again. The time she'd spent yesterday, waiting for Hawk to return, had been interminable.

The sense of dread wouldn't go away. It made her think that if Hawk left her again today, he wouldn't return.

TWELVE

The hurt, disappointment and despair in Jillian's green eyes made him feel like a jerk. He understood where she was coming from, but it wasn't as if he and Ryker were going to hurt Yonkers's sister, Olivia Habush.

Hawk chose to believe that finding Olivia lived in Madison, less than an hour from their cabin motel, was an indication they were on the right track. That this next step was meant to be. Maybe even a sign that God was showing them the way.

He'd begun to realize the importance of having faith and believing that God was watching over them.

Additionally, there was a remote possibility that Yonkers was staying with his sister, or someplace close by, not caring that his actions could place Olivia in danger. Or maybe too arrogant to believe he'd be discovered.

"Please don't do this," Jillian said in a husky whisper. "I can't bear the thought of putting more innocent lives at risk. There has to be another way."

Hawk didn't want to upset Jillian but knew they were running out of time. *He* was running out of time. His shoulder wound was worse today. Not only was it throbbing like crazy, but the edges of the wound were red and puffy. He knew there was an infection brewing deep within.

It wouldn't be long before he'd be too sick to keep Jillian and Lizzy safe.

"I promise we won't hurt her," Ryker spoke up. "That's not the kind of soldiers we are. We were trained to keep innocents safe from harm, and that includes Yonkers's little sister."

Jillian's pleading gaze drilled into Hawk's as if Ryker hadn't spoken. "It's not just that. I'm afraid of losing you, too, Hawk. You and the others helping us."

He didn't think it would help to point out that he would do whatever it took, even putting his own life on the line, to save her life and Lizzy's. "I know. But once we talk with Yonkers, we'll have what we need to put this issue to rest once and for all. This will all be over soon. Just another twenty-four to forty-eight hours."

Jillian pressed her lips together in a tight line. "Forty-eight hours brings us to Christmas Eve. Is this how you want to spend your first Christmas with your daughter? On the run from the bad guys? Doesn't Lizzy deserve something better?"

Ryker shifted uncomfortably in his seat as the disagreement turned personal. He abruptly stood and made his way to the door. "I'll—uh, leave you two alone for a bit. I need to check the perimeter, anyway."

Before Hawk could say anything, Ryker disappeared outside, closing the door firmly behind him. Hawk couldn't blame the guy for ditching them. This was between him and Jillian.

He rose to his feet and stepped closer to his wife, wishing he dared to pull her into his arms. But her defensive stance warned him off.

"I need you to trust me on this, Jillian," he finally said. "I need more information before bringing my case forward to the authorities."

"Need or want?" Her tone was full of challenge.

"Both," he admitted. "I told you before, it's not easy to hide from men in power. If Senator Barton spins some tale that makes it look like I'm the bad guy, I'll be tossed in jail or killed. They've already tried to silence me once. No reason to think they won't do it again."

"But you know more now," she persisted. "You've put some of the puzzle pieces together. Can't Mike or Matt Callahan help protect you? They're cops, aren't they?"

Hawk suppressed a sigh. It wasn't that long ago that Mike was in trouble himself, and being a cop hadn't saved him. In fact, each of the Callahan siblings had overcome adversity over the past couple of years. Unfortunately, he knew only too well that there was a dark side to law enforcement and within the government.

No one was immune to greed.

And the photo of Yonkers selling weapons to the enemy proved it.

"Soon," he promised. "When we have more than an old photo and my fragmented memories to go on, we'll turn everything over to the police. Or maybe the FBI." The idea of going to the federal government had been nagging at him for a while now. The locals didn't have jurisdiction over crimes committed overseas. But the Bureau of Alcohol, Tobacco, Firearms and Explosives did, as well as the Federal Bureau of Investigation.

Maybe he should contact both agencies, just to cover his bases.

"Mommy, I'm hungry."

Lizzy's plaintive tone diverted his attention to his

daughter. She looked adorable, with her pink cheeks and hair messy from sleep.

"Let's use the bathroom first, okay?" Jillian left the kitchen to take care of Lizzy.

While they were in the bathroom, he rummaged for something to make for breakfast. There was more oatmeal, and the hard-boiled eggs Jillian had made yesterday. Worked for him, but he suspected Ryker may want something more substantial.

They could stop by a grocery store on their way to Madison. He quickly made two bowls of oatmeal and peeled two hard-boiled eggs.

Ryker returned as Jillian and Lizzy were eating. Hawk told him they'd stop for something to eat along the way, and Ryker nodded in agreement.

"Everything okay?" Ryker asked in a low tone.

"For now." Hawk knew things wouldn't be okay until the danger was over. "Find anything outside?"

Ryker shook his head. "It's all clear. But I have news. I called Mike and Matt and they're going to be here within the hour."

"Good." Hawk liked the idea of Matt Callahan and Duchess watching over Jillian and Lizzy.

"Listen, I think we should convince Mike to stay here, too," Ryker added. "We've been here for two days now, and that's a long time to stay in one place."

Hawk understood Ryker's reasoning. Staying in one place for too long would eventually expose them to danger. Sure, they'd used disposable phones and a satellite computer, but a senator wielding enormous power could infiltrate any precautions.

"We'll check out other places to stay while we drive," he agreed.

"As soon as the Callahans arrive, we need to hit the road," Ryker said.

Hawk glanced over at Jillian, who was wiping oatmeal off Lizzy's face and hands. "Yeah, I hear you," she said without looking him in the eye.

"Let's get you changed," she told Lizzy, taking her into the bedroom.

Hawk hated the tension widening the gulf between them. But not enough to change his mind about what he and Ryker needed to do.

They had to find Colin Yonkers. No matter what it took.

Jillian wanted to scream in frustration when Hawk and Ryker left the cabin, leaving Mike and Matt Callahan to babysit.

Lizzy was thrilled to see Duchess, the only bright spot of the day.

Ignoring the men hovering in the kitchen, she played Go Fish with Lizzy. The way Mike and Matt exchanged glances she could tell they knew she was upset, but they had no idea how to deal with it. She understood that Hawk's plan wasn't their fault, but they hadn't even tried to talk him out of going to see Colin Yonkers's sister.

As an only child she could only imagine what it was like to have siblings, but she highly doubted that any sister would turn on her brother.

This was nothing more than a fool's errand. One she hoped and prayed didn't turn deadly.

Thirty minutes later, Jillian's anger and frustration faded. She had never been good at holding a grudge. And when she had Lizzy settled on the sofa watching a Disney movie, she returned to the kitchen.

"What can I do to help?"

Mike raised his eyebrows as Matt hid a smile. "You're helping by letting us stay here."

"That's not enough. I'm too restless to sit around like this. There has to be something I can do to assist with the investigation. I may not be a computer whiz, but I can still help with whatever you're searching for."

Again the men exchanged a look that made her grind her teeth with annoyance.

"Why not?" Mike finally said, turning the computer toward her. "We've been searching for photos of Senator Barton and Colin Yonkers. So far, we've only found one of them together."

She remembered seeing the picture last evening. "Did you find a picture of Colin's sister, Olivia?"

"Yes." Matt took over the computer keyboard so he could bring up the picture they'd found on a social media site. "Don't worry about Olivia. Ryker and Hawk won't hurt her."

She truly wanted to believe that. Scrolling through the photographs, she stumbled across one that brought her up short.

"Wait a minute. Who is this guy?" She pointed to a man sitting next to Olivia with his arm around her shoulders.

"Probably her husband," Mike offered. He leaned close to see the image more clearly. "Her last name is Habush, so it stands to reason she's married."

Jillian stared at the image for a long time. Something about the guy nagged at her. He looked familiar. But where would she have seen him?

"I can find his first name easily enough." Matt once again took over the keyboard while Jillian searched her memory. It was there, just out of reach. She'd seen that man before.

"His name is Timothy Habush," Matt announced. "Seems they have a son, Aaron."

The memory clicked into place.

"That's it! He came to Brookland Elementary, claimed he had a son named Aaron going into second grade. Asked the principal if he could watch my class for a while." Jillian couldn't believe she hadn't remembered sooner. "But according to this social media page, his son is only three years old. He lied." The sick feeling in her stomach intensified. "He's a part of this. Maybe he was one of the soldiers in the Alpha team. We need to call Hawk and Ryker to warn them." She fumbled for her disposable phone, but Mike already had his cell in his hand.

"Hawk? Where are you?" Mike demanded.

Jillian held her breath, wishing he'd place the call on speaker.

"Good, stay put. We're coming out to meet you. We have new information that will impact your visit to Yonkers's sister." There was a pause as Mike listened. "I know you don't want them in danger, but this is important. Just stay where you are, we'll meet up with you soon."

"Where are they?" She pounced on Mike the moment he disconnected from the call. "Did they already meet up with Olivia Habush?"

Mike held up his hands. "No, they actually just finished breakfast and were about to head out when I caught them. Apparently they were planning their strategy over steak and eggs."

Jillian felt dizzy with relief. "Good. That's good. Let's go."

"Hold on, Jillian." Matt placed a hand on her arm to stop her. "There's no reason for all of us to go."

"I'm not staying here alone." Jillian narrowed her gaze. "We're all going, understand?"

"She's right," Mike interjected. "I don't want to leave her without a vehicle. Besides, we may need a different strategy altogether. Let's just head to the restaurant and figure out where to go from there."

Jillian didn't waste time. She had Lizzy bundled up for the trip, her Belle doll and teddy bear along for comfort.

As Mike drove, she replayed the day she'd met Timothy Habush at the elementary school.

Why had he come to her classroom? To scope out where she taught? Had he been one of the ski-masked men who'd come to her house that day?

She pressed a hand to her racing heart. It was a good thing she'd insisted on helping, or Hawk and Ryker may have walked into a deadly trap.

Sitting at the family restaurant, waiting for Jillian, Lizzy, Mike and Matt to arrive, chafed at Hawk's nerves. Logically he knew Mike wouldn't have called if it wasn't urgent, but he still resented the Callahans for dragging Jillian and Lizzy along.

They were so close to finding out the truth. Madison was just fifteen minutes away. They could be in and out with a location for Colin Yonkers before anyone was the wiser.

"Here they are now," Ryker commented.

"About time." Hawk knew he sounded grumpy. "This better be good."

He and Ryker had asked for a table large enough to

seat all of them comfortably, including a booster seat for Lizzy. When everyone was settled and had fresh coffee, Hawk pinned Mike with a glare.

"What's going on?"

"Olivia's husband Timothy Habush came to visit my school last week," Jillian said. "The day after I made the call to Fort Bragg."

"What? Are you sure?" Hawk couldn't believe what Jillian was telling him.

"I'm sure. We found his picture on social media." Jillian took a sip of her coffee. "He claimed he had a son named Aaron going into second grade and asked to watch my class for a few minutes. But he lied. His son is three, not seven."

"So he's a part of this." Hawk was dumbfounded. This was an unexpected twist. One, he realized grimly, he should have anticipated.

"Tim Habush," Ryker repeated, his forehead wrinkled in a frown. "I can't place the name."

"Me, either, but that doesn't mean he wasn't part of Team Alpha." Hawk thought about it for a moment. "Or maybe a different team."

"What do you mean?" Ryker asked.

He shrugged. "Think about it. Yonkers wasn't in charge of the Alpha team, but he could have just as easily been coordinating the gun sales with another team. Not Bravo, because I was in charge there and we were friends, but another one."

"I brought the computer." Mike pulled it out and set it on the table. "We can try to poke into Habush's background."

"Not here," Hawk said quickly, glancing around the restaurant. At ten in the morning, it wasn't jam-packed, but he still felt as if they were too exposed, too noticeable. "There's a motel across the street. Let's move there."

"Fine with me," Ryker said, pulling cash out of his pocket and tossing it on the table. "Let's go."

"I want pancakes," Lizzy announced.

Hawk glanced at her in surprise. For a moment he'd forgotten she was sitting beside him. "Sure thing. We'll order you some pancakes to go."

The order didn't take long, and soon they were back outside and across the street at the Family Inn Motel. They rented a room and crowded into it.

Jillian set Lizzy up on the bed with her pancakes and cartoons. When Jillian returned to sit beside him, he put his arm around her shoulders and gave her a quick hug.

"Nice work recognizing Habush. It's another angle to investigate."

"Makes me wonder if there are two teams after us." She frowned. "Maybe Habush is the guy who tossed the classroom looking for the photos, while others came to my house."

Hawk shrugged. "Anything is possible, but I think they're all one and the same."

"Found him," Ryker announced. "Hawk was right. Habush was the team leader for Delta. In fact, I think Duncan O'Hare might have been on Team Delta, too."

Hawk leaned over to see the computer screen for himself. "Does Habush work for Blake-Moore, as well?" He knew Duncan O'Hare didn't, because he was also a Milwaukee cop, like Matt Callahan.

"You got it." Ryker tapped the screen. "All roads lead to Blake-Moore. I still think I could infiltrate the company. Or we could ask Duncan for help."

It wasn't a bad plan, but Hawk knew there wasn't

enough time. His shoulder felt as if it were on fire. "We can still go to the Habush home and convince Olivia to talk."

"And if her husband is there? Along with Yonkers? Then what?" Jillian clearly didn't like the idea.

"We can do a little recon, first," Ryker said in a placating tone. "We don't even know if anyone is home."

"I like that idea." Hawk wanted, needed to keep moving. "We'll check things out and then let you know what we find." He looked at the Callahans. "I need you to stay here."

"I'm coming with you," Mike said quickly. "Matt and Duchess can keep an eye on Jillian and Lizzy."

"I agree." Jillian's comment surprised him. "I'd rather there were three of you in case you run into trouble."

"We're only checking things out," Hawk reminded her.

"Yes, but no one knows we're here," she argued. "We just arrived ten minutes ago. Please take Mike with you."

"Hey, what am I? Chopped liver?" Matt asked. "Don't forget, I am a cop."

Hawk put his hand on Matt's shoulder. "I'm trusting you and Duchess to keep the two most important people in my life safe from harm."

All hint of humor fled from Matt's gaze. "I know. We'll be fine."

Hawk rose to his feet and gestured toward the door. "Time to go."

Mike and Ryker followed him out into the cold winter air. The sky overhead was cloudy, but not enough to indicate snow was on the way.

He let Ryker drive. Ryker drove past the Habush

home, but there were no lights on and no vehicles in the driveway, leading him to believe no one was home.

"We need to get closer." He leaned forward, trying to get a glimpse of the back of the house as Ryker made a circle around the block. "Drop me off here."

"Why don't you let me go?" Mike offered.

"This is my problem." Hawk pushed open the passenger-side door before Mike or Ryker could argue further.

The cold air made him shiver, or maybe it was the fever he was fighting off. Using evergreens for cover, he inched past the house and into the backyard of the Habush home.

He froze when he noticed the back door of the home was hanging ajar. Not good, considering it was late December.

Moving silently, he approached the house. When he was close enough to a window, he peered inside.

A kitchen chair was lying on the floor, amid broken tableware.

Had the place been ransacked, like Jillian's home had been?

And if so, why? What in the world was going on?

THIRTEEN

Jillian found it impossible to sit still, but every time she tried to pace Duchess would wind between her legs, to the point she kept tripping over the beautiful German shepherd.

"Here, Duchess." Lizzy patted the bed. The K-9 gracefully jumped up and snuggled in next to her.

Worrying about Hawk was useless. He had plenty of support between Ryker and Mike, not to mention being a highly trained special ops soldier. He was much stronger and more dangerous than anyone she'd ever met. Yet earlier this morning she'd noticed his face looked pale and drawn, and she'd caught him massaging his injured shoulder whenever he thought no one was looking.

How much longer before he'd agree to go to the hospital for treatment? She feared that delaying medical care would end up causing more damage to the injured muscles in the long run.

But Hawk was stubborn. More so than James had been.

She prayed for Hawk's, Mike's and Ryker's safety, and for Olivia's, too. She trusted the men not to do anything rash, but it was still difficult for her to believe that questioning Yonkers's younger sister was their only option. She couldn't help thinking of Olivia and her three-year-old son, Aaron.

Not so different from her and Lizzy.

"Mommy, look! *The Grinch Who Stole Christmas* is on!"

She turned in time to see the green-faced Grinch scowling from the television screen. "That's great, Lizzy."

"That's Rory's favorite show," Matt spoke up. "He would watch it every day if we let him."

She was curious about the Callahan family who were apparently the only friends, beside Ryker Tillman and Duncan O'Hare, that Hawk had. "How old is Rory?" she asked.

"Three and a half," Matt answered. "He'll be four in February."

"Lizzy will be five in March." She sat down beside Matt. "I can't believe she'll start kindergarten next year. She's ready, but I'm not."

"I know, they grow up fast." Matt scratched Duchess behind the ears. There was a moment of silence before he continued, "I want you to know Hawk has been very supportive of the entire Callahan family over the past couple of years. We'll have his back on this until we get to the bottom of whatever is going on. We all owe him a huge debt of gratitude."

"Thanks. That means a lot to me." She stared down at her hands. When Hawk had brought the jewelry box to the cabin motel, she'd slipped the diamond ring back on the fourth finger of her left hand along with the plain gold band. She'd thought he'd say something, but he hadn't. Or if he had noticed the rings, he didn't let on.

Finally she lifted her gaze to Matt's. "Hawk is different from the man I married."

Matt frowned. "Because of his scar?"

"No, I don't care about that." She waved an impatient hand. "The scar only adds to the air of mystery around him. Do you know he lived next door to me for five months and I never once suspected that he was James?"

Matt lifted a brow in surprise. "Why do you think that is?"

"Well, for one thing, it never occurred to me that my husband wasn't actually dead. But I think it's even more than that. Hawk is more intense. Less talkative." She couldn't seem to put her feelings into words. "I can't explain it, but he's different. In so many little ways."

"I can understand that, but deep down, he's the same man with the same values." Matt shrugged. "It's not that different for me. Rory is my son in every way, except biologically. He is actually my wife Lacy's nephew. Lacy's sister was murdered, so she was forced to go on the run with Rory to keep him safe. Once we found out who killed her, we were able to formally adopt Rory. He was about nine months old. But even without the paperwork, I always felt as if he was my own flesh and blood. Lacy is pregnant, and I can't imagine loving the new baby any differently from Rory."

"Wow, I had no idea." She glanced at Lizzy, realizing her daughter's situation was almost the exact opposite. Hawk was biologically Lizzy's father but hadn't been a part of her life over the past four years.

Until now.

Once the danger was over, she and Hawk needed to talk about the future. The idea of going back to living in separate houses, even if they were right next door to each other, wasn't good enough.

She wanted more. She wanted it all.

The engagement ring glittered on her left hand next to the gold wedding band. She wanted a family.

Hawk pushed the door of the Habush home open while remaining plastered against the side of the house, his Glock held ready.

He had no idea what he might find upon going inside.

It was likely no one was in there, but he refused to make rash assumptions. He was beginning to think Jillian had pegged it correctly when she suggested there was more than one team after them.

Why else would one team turn on the other?

The back door opened into the kitchen. He silently entered the house, avoiding the broken bits scattered across the floor. Keeping his back to the wall, he ventured further inside.

He frowned when he found the living room apparently untouched. Nothing seemed to have been disturbed.

The place hadn't been ransacked, after all. Clearly something had gone down in the kitchen, though.

And where were Olivia and Aaron Habush?

After clearing the living room, Hawk made his way down the hallway to the bedrooms. Those rooms hadn't been disturbed, either, although they appeared more lived in. There was a master bedroom and a kid's room, judging by the train motif. Clothes were strewn about in the child's bedroom, giving Hawk the impression they'd left in a hurry.

Why? And what had happened in the kitchen?

He poked his head one last time in the master bedroom, searching for a clue behind what had transpired here. There was a framed photograph on the bedside table. He crossed over to pick it up, to examine it more closely.

The photo was a family picture of Tim, Olivia and Aaron Habush.

There was something about Habush that nagged at him. But when he tried to think back to his time in Afghanistan, he couldn't place the guy. Either because of the holes in his memory or because he hadn't interacted with him very much. The fact that Habush was the leader of the Delta team made him fear it was his memory.

Which brought him back to the possibility that his brief memory around Senator Rick Barton wasn't accurate, either. Every last bit of circumstantial evidence they had all pointed to the Blake-Moore mercenary group.

After replacing the photo where he'd found it, Hawk moved back to the kitchen. He stared at the scene for several long moments, trying to imagine what had transpired.

Remnants of breakfast food were on the table, bits of scrambled eggs and bacon. He crossed over and felt the coffeepot: it was still slightly warm. Glancing back at the table, he noted one of the chairs had a booster seat, no doubt used by the little boy, Aaron. The broken dishes were on the floor near the overturned chair, which was right next to Aaron's booster seat. Seemed logical that Olivia might have been the one sitting beside her son.

Only two plates and one broken coffee cup. Did that mean Tim hadn't been here before they left? That he'd burst into the kitchen to grab his wife because he was in a hurry to leave? So much so that he hadn't bothered to make sure the door was closed and locked behind him?

Had Olivia resisted for some reason? Maybe leaving the back door open as a warning sign that something bad had happened?

There was a scrap of paper on the floor, half buried by a broken piece of a plate. Hawk picked it up. It was a receipt for gas purchased last week.

The location of the gas station was near Brookland Elementary. He clenched his jaw, even though the receipt didn't tell him anything new. Jillian had already identified Tim as being at the school the day after she'd called Fort Bragg about the envelope Hawk had sent her.

But it gave him an idea. He opened kitchen cabinets and drawers until he found one full of paperwork. When he rifled through them, he found more credit card receipts.

Scanning the purchases, he felt adrenaline surge through his bloodstream. There were several charges for gas, and he found one that had been made near the area of his cabin.

Tim Habush was part of the team in coming after them at the cabin—that much was clear. And likely in on the gunrunning, as well. But that didn't explain why he'd taken his wife and son and bolted out of their home.

He took every single receipt he could find, stuffing them deep into his pockets so he could review them more closely later. At least the gas receipt put Tim Habush near his cabin and provided a connection to Yonkers.

Still, it wasn't enough, and as Hawk slipped back out of the house and back toward the SUV where Mike and Ryker waited, he wondered why these guys were always a step ahead of him.

When he stepped outside, he came up short when he

sensed someone nearby. He lifted his Glock, then slowly lowered it when he recognized Ryker.

"You were gone for a long time," Ryker said. "I've been covering the back, and Mike is out front."

Hawk should have expected his buddies wouldn't simply sit and wait. "Thanks, but there isn't anyone inside."

Ryker nodded. "What did you find?"

Tillman's keen perception made him smile. "Let's get back to the motel where we left Matt and Jilly. I'll show you what I have."

Ryker didn't argue. "Stay here. I'll get Mike."

When Ryker moved to the front of the house, Hawk looked down at the ground, looking for tell-tale signs of a struggle, mentally kicking himself for not checking sooner. Still, he could see where he'd come in but couldn't tell between Ryker's boot prints and several others.

He was losing his touch. Sure, maybe it was the infection developing in his shoulder, but the moment he'd noticed the back door was open, he should have scouted the ground for clues.

His gaze narrowed on several broken tips of a bush beside the house. There was a hint of blue thread on the tip, maybe from denim jeans.

It was looking more and more like Olivia and Aaron were hauled out of here against their will. He just wished he understood why.

"Hawk? You okay?"

Hawk turned to face Ryker and Mike who had both been inside the house. "Yeah, I'm fine. Let's get out of here."

The trip back to the motel didn't take long. Jillian ran to him as he entered the room.

"Hawk! Is everything all right?"

He knew she was mostly concerned about Olivia and her son. "The house was empty," he quickly informed her. "But it looks as if they left in a hurry. And maybe not of their own volition."

Jillian paled. "What do you mean?"

Hawk described the scene in the kitchen as he pulled crumpled receipts from his pockets and dumped them on the small table. "I can't explain why Olivia's husband or her brother would drag her out of there like that. It doesn't make any sense."

"What's all this?" Matt began straightening the receipts.

"Found one for a gas station near Brookland Elementary on the same day Jillian saw Tim Habush checking out the second-grade classroom. And then another one for gas several days later, only this time it was a station not far from my cabin. So I grabbed all of them to see what else we can link together with what has been happening."

They spread the receipts out and began reviewing them. Hawk found a third receipt for a fast-food restaurant near Jillian's house. The date stamp was for Friday, the same day her home had been breached by two masked men.

He thought it was possible Tim Habush and Colin Yonkers had been staked out nearby, watching Jillian's house until it was time to make their move.

"Wait a minute, do you notice that none of these receipts are for anything past Saturday?" Jillian spoke up.

"I have two from Friday," Hawk said, lifting them up for her to see. "This is three total, all near places you and I have been."

"But none are more recent." Jillian scowled. "It's almost as if Tim Habush hasn't been home since Friday."

At that moment it clicked. The reason Tim Habush's photo had nagged at him back at the house.

It was the man he'd unmasked at Jillian's house. The same one he'd recognized outside his cabin.

Tim Habush was dead.

Hawk had shot him in self-defense.

Jillian caught the flash of horror in Hawk's gaze and instinctively knew what he was thinking.

"He was one of them, wasn't he?" she asked softly. "Up at the cabin."

Hawk slowly nodded. "He's dead. He shot at me, so I returned fire."

Jillian's heart ached for Hawk. A woman she didn't know was a widow, her son fatherless. She felt bad for Olivia and Aaron Habush, yet knew Hawk hadn't wanted to hurt anyone. The way he'd left the men alive at her house proved it.

But that hadn't prevented him from doing whatever was necessary to save her and Lizzy.

Hawk abruptly stood, pushing away from the table. The space inside the room was cramped and she could tell he wanted to get out.

"We need to head back to the cabin motel." He avoided looking at anyone directly. "We'll stay one more night, then find somewhere else to go."

"Why not just stay here?" Ryker asked.

"Um, there aren't enough rooms open," Mike spoke up. "No connecting rooms for sure. When I paid for this room, the manager told me that there was only one other vacant room on the other side of the building. I guess it must be too close to the holiday."

"We need to make sure the cabin is wiped down anyway," Hawk said, hovering near the door. "And my antibiotics are still there, along with my supplies."

"You're feeling worse, aren't you?" Jillian stepped forward and placed her hand on Hawk's forehead. His skin was hot to the touch. Cold fingers of fear squeezed her heart. If anything happened to Hawk...

"I'm okay, but I need those antibiotics." Hawk pulled away from her touch and opened the door to the motel room. "Let's go."

Jillian wanted to argue but concentrated on bundling Lizzy into her winter coat as the men quickly filed out of the room. She was troubled by Hawk's illness and tried to think of a compromise.

Originally she hadn't wanted to be left with the Callahans while he worked the case. But that was before she'd gotten to know them. Mike and Matthew were both decent men, as was Ryker Tillman. She needed to convince Hawk to turn everything over to the authorities and assure him that the Callahans could keep her safe while he received treatment for his injury at the hospital.

Even if they didn't get to the bottom of this right away, they could start up again after the holidays. And once Hawk was feeling better.

Hawk came back to the room, looking impatient as he waited for her.

"We're ready." She carried Lizzy to the door.

"I'll take her," Hawk offered. Lizzy didn't mind when Hawk gently pulled her away. "We'll go to the cabin for a few hours, but Mike and Matt are going to search for a new place for us to stay. They promise to find something kid-friendly."

"Okay." She liked the way Hawk held Lizzy against his chest, clutching her teddy bear with her small head tucked beneath his chin.

The trip back to the cabin motel didn't take long. She was all too aware that the first thing Hawk did was to find the bottle of antibiotics. He downed the pills, chasing them with a large glass of water. Then he added a couple of ibuprofens and took those, too.

While he cleaned the place up, no doubt getting rid of any and all evidence of their staying there, she went into the bedroom to pack up Lizzy's things.

A strange thumping noise coming from outside made her frown. What in the world? It almost sounded like…

A helicopter?

For a moment she was paralyzed with fear, then found the strength to take immediate action.

"Come with me, Lizzy." She held Lizzy close and rushed into the kitchen. The thump, thump, thumping noise grew louder.

"Hawk! A helicopter!"

Hawk joined her a split second later, glancing around the room. "Where's Ryker?"

She shook her head helplessly. "I don't know. I don't think he came inside with us."

Hawk grabbed the car keys off the table and crossed over to the door. "We have to get out of here. Hurry!"

"We can't outdrive a helicopter," she protested. It took her a moment to pull on her winter coat and Lizzy's too, before following him outside.

The chopper was coming in from the north, fast and

low, looking like a dark menacing bird of prey about to pounce.

"Hurry!" Hawk shouted, staying behind her as they made their way toward the SUV.

But even as he spoke, four men, dressed completely in black and with rifles slung over their shoulders, emerged from the helicopter. They rappelled down until they were on the ground and quickly came toward them.

Jillian froze, holding Lizzy tightly against her chest as the little girl sobbed with fright.

They were surrounded!

FOURTEEN

Ryker had been right. They never should have come back to the cabin motel. As Hawk turned to face the men, all four strategically standing in a semicircle around them, with the SUV at their backs, Hawk pushed Jillian and Lizzy protectively behind him. Then he raised his hands up in a gesture of surrender.

The only possible source of rescue would be from Ryker. Hawk didn't have a clue where he was but knew the soldier would have heard the chopper. He hoped and prayed Ryker was hiding in the woods, getting ready to make his move at a strategic time.

"You want me? Fine." Hawk hoped these men couldn't hear the hint of desperation in his tone. Lizzy's crying wrenched at his heart, but he did his best to ignore it. "You've got me. Now let the woman and child go. They don't know anything, I'm the one you came for."

The four armed men didn't say anything but stood in place as if waiting for something.

Or someone.

The SUV was only about thirty feet away. Thirty feet that may as well have been thirty miles.

He never should have come back here. If Jillian and

Lizzy died today, it would be his fault. He could hear Jillian trying to reassure Lizzy, even though the situation was bad. Worse than bad.

He sent up a desperate prayer that God would keep his wife and daughter safe from harm.

"Let them go," Hawk repeated. "I'll come with you without a struggle once they're safe in the SUV and have driven far from here."

Still no response from the four men. Clearly they were waiting for their next order. From whom, he didn't know.

Yonkers? Or higher brass within the Blake-Moore group?

He scanned their faces. At least they weren't wearing ski masks this time. Hawk tried to search his fragmented memory for recognition. It was highly likely that one or more of them had served with him in Afghanistan.

But he couldn't place a single one. They were strangers to him. Strangers that wouldn't hesitate to put a bullet through his heart.

"I'm not leaving without you," Jillian whispered.

He ignored her because it wasn't her decision. Hawk tried to come up with an escape plan. With Ryker's help, he thought they might be able to take out all four of them, giving Jillian and Lizzy the chance to get away unharmed. The only problem was that his and Ryker's chances of surviving such a rash attempt were slim to none.

Didn't matter. Nothing was more important than keeping Jillian and Lizzy safe. And he sensed Ryker would feel the same way.

He remembered what Ryker had said about not hurting Olivia and Aaron because that was not the kind of soldiers they were. They were wired to protect the innocent. Especially women and children.

He could trust Ryker to keep Jillian and Lizzy safe.

The sound of movement coming through the trees snagged his attention. He tensed, ready to make his move.

When a familiar figure came through the trees, surprisingly alone, Hawk knew he shouldn't have been surprised.

Senator Rick Barton.

His memory hadn't been wrong. He had seen Major Rick Barton in the Afghan mountains five years ago.

Realizing the senator was the one behind all of this made Hawk sick to his stomach. He should have sent all of his evidence to the FBI or the CIA.

Now it was too late.

"Hello, James."

Hawk didn't answer, partially because there was a lump in his throat the size of Mount Rushmore.

"I know you may find this difficult to believe but I'm here to help," the senator continued. "You've stumbled into a bit of a mess, wouldn't you agree?"

Hawk stared at Barton without responding. He wasn't buying the oh-so-innocent act. Senators didn't come after a soldier with a chopper full of armed men.

Not unless the mission was to silence a threat.

"We don't have a lot of time, James." The senator's easygoing tone now held a hard edge. "So let me sum things up for you. I know you witnessed a gun deal five years ago outside of Kabul between Colin Yonkers, an American soldier, and the insurgents. I know that the plane carrying the Bravo team was sabotaged and crashed in the Appalachian Mountains. I know your body was never found and I always suspected you'd turn up one day. And finally I know you have proof of the gun deal." Barton paused for a moment, then spread his hands wide. "That covers just about everything, doesn't it?"

A strained silence hung between them for a long moment. Hawk knew that a prolonged silence often made others want to talk to fill in the gap, but Rick Barton had been trained the same way he had been.

No one spoke or moved a fraction of an inch.

"Not even close." Hawk finally said in a harsh tone. "You forgot to mention how you sent armed men in ski masks to my wife's house. How you ordered her home to be ransacked along with her classroom in an effort to find the proof I currently have in my possession. How you also sent four men after us at my cabin, but only three survived." Hawk took a moment to meet the gazes of each of the four men. "I guess that soldier didn't mean much to you, as I see you've replaced him easily enough. Tell me, are they all willing to die for you the way Tim Habush did?"

"Those weren't my soldiers," Barton protested. "I'm telling you, I'm not the one out to hurt you. If you'll just come with me to Washington, DC, then we can straighten this out."

Yeah, right, Hawk thought snidely. He knew if he went with the senator there was no way he'd actually make it to Washington, DC alive. More likely they'd shove him out of the chopper to his death where it would take weeks, maybe even months, before his body was found.

But if he could buy some time for Ryker to get Jillian and Lizzy to safety, it might be worth it. He wished he knew exactly where Ryker was. And he wished he'd never allowed Mike and Matt Callahan to go out ahead of them to find a new place to stay.

His mistakes might result in the deaths of his wife and daughter. And that couldn't be tolerated.

"Here are my terms. I'll go with you back to DC, if you'll let Jillian and Lizzy go."

"No." Jillian spoke out loud for the first time since the armed men had all but surrounded them. "We're not leaving without you, Hawk."

"Hawk?" Like a rattlesnake finding a mouse in the grass, the senator pounced on his new name. "Is that the name you're going by these days? No wonder it was so difficult to find you."

The new name had helped keep him under the radar. If he hadn't sent Jillian those stupid photographs all those years ago, they wouldn't have found him now. Hawk couldn't stand knowing that this mess was his fault.

As he stared Rick Barton down, he tried to plan his next move. Because he wasn't going to let Jillian and Lizzy suffer because of his choices.

"Let Jillian and Lizzy go," he repeated. "Once they're far enough away that they can't be seen, I'll go with you to DC. That's my offer. Take it or leave it."

The senator's smile was humorless. "You seem to think you're in a position to negotiate, James. But you're not."

Hawk's muscles tensed. He hoped and prayed Ryker was nearby, l-istening to the conversation, ready to jump in to help get Jillian and Lizzy to safety as needed. The moment the senator flinched, he'd make his move.

"But since I'm not the one behind all of this, I'm happy to oblige," Barton said as if he were giving Hawk a medal instead of a death sentence. "Maybe then you'll realize that my only concern is getting to the bottom of the gun dealing in Afghanistan. So sure, go ahead." Barton waved a dismissive hand. "The woman and child are free to go."

"No," Jillian protested, her voice loud enough to be heard over Lizzy's crying. "I'm not leaving you."

"Yes, you are." He turned to give her a steely glare. "Hurry. I need you and Lizzy to be safe."

Her eyes pleaded with his, but he refused to budge. Finally she nodded and hitched Lizzy higher in her arms.

"Reach out to the Callahans," he murmured in a low voice, hoping the armed men wouldn't hear beyond Lizzy's sobs. "They'll help you."

Jillian gave a slight nod to indicate she got the message. She took several steps backward, until she was near the SUV. After securing Lizzy in her car seat, she walked around and slid in behind the wheel. The entire process seemed interminably slow, but Jillian finally had the car in gear and began rumbling down the driveway.

He watched, memorizing the way she looked, hoping it wouldn't be the last time he'd see her, before he turned to face Barton.

The moment Jillian and Lizzy were no longer in danger, Hawk sensed the tension between the gunmen relaxed. Maybe Lizzy's crying had gotten on their nerves, too. Either way, they no long perceived him as a threat.

That was their mistake.

"Ready?" the senator asked.

Hawk didn't move. "Not until she's out of sight." He didn't dare rake a gaze around the area to find Ryker's position. The guy was either out there ready to help, or he wasn't.

Hawk hoped and prayed it wasn't the latter.

* * *

Jillian couldn't believe Hawk had stayed behind with the senator. She should have known he was right all along. Men in power could do whatever they wanted.

Even sending four armed men rappelling down from a helicopter to capture them.

While she'd been partially hidden behind Hawk, she'd dialed 911 from the phone in her pocket. At least, she hoped she had. It wasn't an easy thing to do when you couldn't see the numbers.

But the 911 response wouldn't be quick enough. Not considering they were way out here in the middle of no-where. By the time the sheriff's deputies arrived, Barton and his armed men would be long gone.

Taking Hawk with them.

She considered calling again but didn't think that would create a faster response. However, remember-ing the phone gave her an idea. She slowed the SUV, twisted in her seat and used the disposable phone she'd been given to snap a quick picture of Hawk standing with his spine ramrod straight and staring at Barton while surrounded by four armed men. If anything happened to him, she wanted proof of what had gone down here.

Leaving Hawk at Barton's mercy caused tears to well in her eyes, blurring her vision. She swiped them away, knowing she needed to drive safe for Lizzy's sake.

But fearing the worst made her heart ache. She couldn't lose Hawk now that she'd found him. She just couldn't!

Please, Lord. Please keep Hawk safe in Your care!

In an attempt to stall for time, she kept her speed slow. Using her phone, she called Mike Callahan, leaving a message when he didn't pick up. Keeping the phone close, she turned her attention back to the rural highway.

Mike returned her call within two minutes. "What's going on?"

"Senator Barton dropped four armed men from a helicopter to surround us. Hawk convinced them to let me and Lizzy drive away in the SUV, but he's back there alone with them. The senator is planning to take Hawk to DC, but I don't believe he'll make it there alive." The words tumbled out in a rush, as fear stabbed deep. "We need to do something."

"Where's Ryker?"

Good question. "I don't know. He wasn't in the cabin when the chopper arrived, so I have to assume he's hiding in the woods somewhere, waiting for the opportunity to help."

"Good. At least Hawk isn't alone."

She wanted to fast-pitch the phone through the windshield. "Didn't you hear me? There are four armed men with the senator! That's five against two!"

"I heard you, Jillian, but you have to have faith in Hawk and Ryker's abilities. They are both highly trained soldiers. And I need you to calm down and be patient. Matt and I will meet you at the gas station just outside Paloma. It's the closest town to the east."

She didn't want to be calm. She wanted them to rush over to help rescue Hawk. She heard Lizzy sniffling in the back seat and managed to pull herself together. "Okay, fine. I'll meet you at the gas station in Paloma."

She disconnected from the call and took several deep breaths in an attempt to calm her racing heart. She unflexed her fingers from their death-like grip on the steering wheel and tried to think rationally.

Mike was probably right about Hawk's and Ryker's skills. At some point during the standoff, she'd hoped Ryker would rush in, guns blazing, to take out the threat. But obviously that would be too dangerous. Not just for her and Lizzy, but for Hawk and Ryker, too.

Maybe now that she and Lizzy were out of the way, they'd find a way to escape. She thought about how Ryker might wait until they were all hiking through the woods back to the chopper. She'd watched Hawk in action enough to know that a surprise attack from an unknown assailant would be their best chance for escape.

Who was she kidding? She wasn't a trained soldier and really had no idea how or when Ryker should make his move.

All she could do was to continue driving Lizzy safely out of harm's way.

And pray.

Hawk waited a full five minutes after Jillian and Lizzy left before he gestured toward the chopper. "Okay, they're safe. Let's go."

Senator Barton looked relieved to have Hawk's cooperation. But that didn't prevent him from instructing one of the armed guards to pat Hawk down.

Hawk tried not to wince as he held his arms out to the side. The bullet wound was throbbing again. He didn't say a word when the gunman relieved Hawk of his weapon and tucked it away.

If Ryker was listening, Hawk hoped he'd take up a position somewhere along the path to the chopper. It wouldn't be easy to take out all four men, but he'd been in worse situations.

It was easier to think clearly now that Jillian and

Lizzy were safe. He was confident the Callahans would protect his wife and daughter.

No point in thinking past the next step. If he didn't return to them, so be it. At this point he was putting his faith in his skills, in Ryker and, most important of all, in God.

He moved toward the opening in the woods exactly where Barton had come out just, what, twenty minutes ago? He could see by the broken branches that the senator had lost his warrior edge.

Which was good. Because Hawk needed to be able to escape from him before they reached the chopper.

"Wait," Barton called before they entered the woods. "Nate and Jackson, you stay in the rear. Wes and Tom, you're behind me. Keep Hawk in the middle just in case he decides to get cute."

Hawk was fairly certain that whatever moves he made to escape weren't going to be considered cute. But he didn't respond as Barton went first, followed closely by Wes and Tom.

They only took about ten steps when Ryker made his move. Hawk was ready. The moment he heard the scuffle behind him, he lashed out at the guy in front of him, hitting him hard on the back of his head while grabbing his weapon.

The man—Wes?—let out a cry before crumpling to the ground. Tom quickly turned to shoot, but Hawk fired first. Tom went down, dropping his weapon. He wasn't dead but curled in a ball, holding a hand to his injured thigh. After double-checking to make sure Wes was still unconscious, Hawk grabbed Tom's weapon and rushed after Barton.

"Stop or I'll shoot," Hawk demanded. He didn't have

to look behind him. He was certain Ryker had done his job with the last two men.

Barton went pale as he lifted his hands in the air. "James, listen to me. You're making a big mistake. I'm trying to help you! There was no reason for you to kill anyone!"

"If you wanted to help me, you shouldn't have come in with a chopper and armed guards," Hawk countered. "So don't bother feeding me that line. I don't believe you. Now we're going to head back to the clearing, nice and slow."

Barton didn't move, and Hawk could tell the senator was weighing his options.

"Now!" Hawk let his impatience show. Maybe because all this fighting had reopened his shoulder wound for what felt like the tenth time. At this rate it would never heal. "Move it."

"Have it your way." Senator Barton took a few steps toward Hawk, clearly not willing to get too close.

Hawk moved to the side and gestured with the weapon for Barton to walk past him. After a few steps, Hawk saw that Ryker had tied Wes, who was groaning as he regained consciousness, and Nate to different trees. Ryker had also tied the two injured men together, as well. He'd taken possession of the weapons, holding one ready, two others looped over each shoulder.

"I have your Glock," Ryker told him.

Hawk gave him a nod. "Thanks." His gratitude was more for coming to the rescue so than for reclaiming his weapon, and Ryker knew it.

Words weren't necessary.

"You're making a big mistake," Barton said again.

"You can't seriously think you're going to get away with killing a senator."

"I'm not going to kill you," Hawk replied in an even tone. "I'm going to make you talk."

"I have been talking! I've told you I'm not the one who is out to hurt you! I want to help! You won't believe me!"

"Keep walking." Hawk stumbled a bit and caught the look of concern Ryker shot in his direction. He wasn't done yet.

They needed information from Barton.

The wail of sirens cutting through the silence made Hawk frown. He hadn't expected such a quick response to the gunfire, considering how far out in the country they were.

"Change of plan," Hawk told Ryker. "Let's get the senator and his men back to his chopper."

"Roger that," Ryker agreed.

"Police sirens," Barton said in what seemed to be relieved surprise. "Good. That's a relief. It means help is on the way."

Good? Relief? Help is on the way? Hawk exchanged a glance with Ryker. Why was the senator glad to hear the police were on their way?

Was it possible that Hawk had it wrong? That the senator really wasn't out to hurt him?

Or was he planning to turn this entire incident back onto Hawk and Ryker?

As the sirens grew louder, Hawk grimly realized they'd soon find out.

FIFTEEN

From her position at the gas station, Jillian could hear the police sirens. Her 911 call had worked! She clenched the steering wheel tightly, hoping and praying Hawk and Ryker were all right.

Moments later, two sheriff's department vehicles drove past. On the heels of that, Mike and Matt Callahan arrived to park beside her. Mike lowered his driver's-side window, and she did the same with the passenger side.

"We're going back to the cabin motel," she announced, leaning over so he could hear her. "The police are headed there, too."

Mike and Matt exchanged a long look that she easily interpreted as not being in favor of her plan.

Too bad. She wasn't taking no for an answer.

"I'm going." She abruptly threw the SUV into Reverse and began backing up away from the parking space.

Mike quickly backed up, too, cutting her off. "Hold on," he shouted. His voice came loudly through their respective open windows. "Let's just wait for a minute, okay? I can't take you anywhere near the line of fire. We need to wait until the sheriff's deputies have the scene under control."

"I don't want to wait." Her voice sounded petulant even to her own ears, so she tried to search for a reasonable alternative. "I promise we'll stay out of danger, but I need to make sure Hawk is okay. Ryker, too. I can't just sit here without knowing."

"Jillian, you're going to get me in trouble with Hawk," Mike said with a heavy sigh.

"I don't care." She wasn't budging on this.

"Okay, you can follow us," Mike said. "We'll go in first. But I'm warning you, I'm going to stop far away from any hint of danger."

"I understand." She couldn't argue, especially since she had Lizzy in the back seat. Even being a little closer would be better than sitting way back here. "Thanks, Mike."

"Yeah." He didn't look happy but continued backing up and then heading out of the gas station first, leaving her to follow.

Jillian raised the window. As she drove, she stayed close to Mike's rear bumper. Seeing Duchess in the K-9 crate area of the SUV was oddly reassuring. It made her realize that they basically were adding three more cops to the attempt to rescue Hawk.

If they weren't too late.

As she followed Mike back up the long, winding road leading to the cabin motel, she watched the sky, hoping, praying she hadn't somehow missed the helicopter taking off. She imagined that if that happened, Hawk would be in the back like some sort of prisoner.

The brake lights flashed on Mike's SUV, causing her to slow to a stop. He slid out from behind the wheel, as did Matt. Matt walked around to let Duchess out. Mike stepped toward her vehicle, holding his hands up as an indication she needed to wait.

She nodded, knowing he and Matt were right to be the ones to go in to find out what was happening. Three cops, she reminded herself. If there was a way to rescue Hawk, she believed the Callahans could do it.

"Mommy? Where are we?"

She twisted in her seat to look back at her daughter. "We're back at the cabin motel. Mr. Mike and Mr. Matt are going to find Daddy."

The word slipped out before she realized what she'd said. Lizzy scrunched up her forehead as if confused. "Daddy?" she echoed.

Jillian regretted she hadn't had this discussion with her daughter sooner. Especially considering the very real possibility that Hawk may not survive whatever was going on in the clearing.

"Yes, Lizzy. Mr. Hawk is your daddy. He was gone for a long time, but now he's back. And he loves you very much."

"Is going to live with us like a family?" Lizzy asked.

That gave her pause. She cleared her throat. "I don't know, we'll have to wait and see."

Lizzy frowned, not liking that answer, but Jillian wouldn't lie to her.

As much as she'd come to care for Hawk, depending on him to keep them safe from harm, she hadn't dwelled too much on their future.

The idea of living with Hawk as husband and wife, as a family, made her aware of the way she'd responded to his kiss. The attraction was still there, at least on her part.

But things were so different now. It simply wasn't

realistic to believe they could just pick up where they'd left off five years ago.

And what did Hawk want to do once the danger was over? She had no idea.

She stared at the diamond engagement ring. Had she put it on prematurely? They needed time to talk. To get to know each other. To find out all the ways they'd both changed.

Before they could even consider what their future might hold.

Hawk gestured to Ryker that Wes and Nate should be placed into the helicopter. "Tie them inside, then get the two injured men, as well. I want them all out of here before the cops arrive."

Ryker nodded and quickly went to work. Hawk wasn't sure what his buddy thought about Senator Barton's response to having heard the police sirens. The senator's reaction continued to nag at him.

"Tell me about Yonkers." Hawk drilled Barton with a steely glare, the tip of his weapon never wavering from the man's chest.

Barton nodded. "I asked you to keep an eye on Yonkers for me. I'd heard some chatter about the guy leaving camp alone and didn't like it. Rumor had it he was up to no good. So I ordered you to keep an eye on him."

Hawk mulled over the senator's claim. "Where were we when we had this conversation?"

"In the mountains." Barton frowned at him. "It's not as if I could have that conversation with you in camp."

Was that the memory that had haunted Hawk all these years? Was that the reason he'd suspected Barton was involved in something illegal? Because they'd had a secret meeting where he'd been ordered to spy on one of his fellow soldiers?

On his friend?

Ryker hauled the first injured soldier into the chopper and went back for the second as if oblivious to the conversation.

But Hawk suspected the former special ops soldier was listening to every word.

"So how is it that you know that the Bravo team's plane was sabotaged?" The sirens were louder now, and Hawk knew they were running out of time. "If you knew we were in danger, why didn't you stop it?"

"I didn't think you were in danger once we had your team stateside," Barton explained. "Yonkers was still in Afghanistan, so I figured it was safe. It wasn't until I heard about the plane going down over the Appalachian Mountains that I realized how badly I'd misjudged the level of corruption. I'm sorry about that."

Sorry? He was sorry that Hawk had lost his entire team? That he'd barely escaped with his own life? That he'd lost four years of being with his wife and daughter?

Sorry didn't begin to cover it.

Ryker tossed the second soldier into the chopper. "The police are getting close," he warned.

"So why not simply arrest Yonkers and be done with it?" Hawk asked. He was torn by indecision. He knew his memory wasn't exactly reliable, but it was difficult for him to buy into the senator's story. Barton wasn't telling the entire truth, although there could be bits and pieces of his story that were correct. But why would Barton have come here with the intent of dragging him back to DC with the help of four armed guards? Who did crazy stuff like that?

"Because Yonkers didn't have the power to bring down your team's plane." Barton finally responded to Hawk's question. "A stunt like that took someone higher up on the command chain than Yonkers. And frankly, I don't know who I can trust." Barton spread his hands wide. "For a while, I suspected you were involved, James. That you had decided to join forces with Yonkers."

"That's ridiculous." Hawk didn't hesitate to protest. "I would never sell out my country for money."

Barton nodded slowly. "I believe you."

"Did you hire the Blake-Moore group?" Hawk asked.

Barton frowned. "No. Who are they?"

"A mercenary group formed by two ex-soldiers. Yonkers works for them." Hawk watched Barton's face carefully for a reaction.

"I don't know anything about them." Barton's expression turned grim. "But maybe I should."

Barton was either an award-winning actor or telling the truth. Hawk couldn't decide which. He glanced at Ryker as if seeking advice. Ryker tipped his head toward the chopper and he understood the soldier's unspoken directive.

"Get out of here," Hawk told the senator.

Before Barton could make a move to get into the helicopter, two deputies burst through the path from the woods. "Police! Drop your weapon!"

Suddenly weary, his shoulder hurting to the point his vision was getting blurry, Hawk slowly did as he was told. He tossed the gun in his hand along with the two AK-47s on the ground and then held his hands out from his sides, palms up. His injury hurt too much to lift them up over his head.

"It's okay, Officers," Barton called out. "I'm Senator Rick Barton. Everything is fine here."

Huh? Hawk wondered if he was becoming delusional from the infection brewing in his shoulder.

The deputies glanced at each other but didn't lower their weapons. "Who called 911?"

Hawk realized it must have been Jillian. Either during their standoff or right after she'd left with Lizzy.

"Not me," he managed to say. "The senator took us by surprise, arriving in a helicopter." He decided to stick to the truth.

"Well, someone did." The deputy wasn't inclined to believe his meager attempt to explain what was happening here. Hawk wasn't entirely sure what was going on, himself. Why was Barton sticking up for them? "And here you are, pointing a weapon at a senator," the deputy said.

"He wasn't pointing a weapon at me. I told you, this is nothing more than a misunderstanding." Barton's voice had taken an authoritative tone.

"That's for someone else to determine," the deputy responded. "For now, we'll take both of these guys into custody."

Ryker hadn't moved from his stance in front of the open chopper door. Hawk wondered if he thought that being there would help hide the fact that there were two bound and two wounded soldiers inside.

"Deputies, if you'll allow me to call Special Agent in Charge Dennis Ludwig at the FBI, I'm sure we can get this cleared up without an issue." Barton reached into his pocket and pulled out a phone.

The deputies looked stunned as they listened to the senator request to speak directly with SAC Ludwig.

After a brief interaction, Barton held the cell phone out toward the deputies. "For you."

The deputy closest to Hawk stepped forward and gingerly took the senator's cell phone. The one-sided conversation was brief. "Yes, sir. I understand, sir. Thank you, sir." The deputy handed the phone back to the senator. "We'll be on our way, now."

"Thank you for your dedicated service to our community." Barton slipped the phone back into his pocket.

The two deputies turned and retraced their steps through the woods, leaving Hawk speechless.

"Why?" Hawk forced the question past his tight throat.

"I tried to tell you. I'm on your side." Barton glanced back at the helicopter. "Obviously, I handled this wrong, and two good men were injured because of it." He swung back to face Hawk. "I'll take responsibility for this mess, but not for sabotaging your plane."

Hawk wasn't sure how to respond.

"Call me on my personal cell when you feel safe." Barton rattled off his number, then abruptly turned and jumped into the back of the chopper.

Taken by surprise, Ryker quickly stepped out of the way.

"Hope to hear from you soon," Barton shouted before giving the pilot the signal. The rotor blades on the top of the chopper began to spin.

Ryker instinctively lowered his head, the same way Hawk did. They retreated to the back of the clearing, watching in stunned surprise as the helicopter rose off the ground.

The whirling blades made too much noise for them

to talk, so they simply waited until the pilot banked the chopper and flew out of sight.

"What just happened?" Hawk finally asked, breaking the silence.

"No clue." Ryker hesitated, then turned back toward the now clearly visible path through the woods. "If Barton's not the one who hired Blake-Moore, then who is? It has to be someone who knew about the gun deal in Afghanistan."

"I have no idea." Hawk didn't like this recent turn of events. It was difficult to wrap his mind around what Barton had said. That the senator had actually prevented him and Ryker from being arrested.

Still, something wasn't right. Even if Barton was one of the good guys, he had a funny way of showing it. He remembered how both Todd Hayes, the current secretary of defense, and Colonel McCann—now known as General McCann—whom Barton and Hayes had reported to, had also served overseas. It could be one of them, or someone else.

Hawk still had no idea whom he could trust.

Jillian waited in the SUV with Lizzy for what seemed like an eternity. What was taking them so long? Finally, Mike came back to talk to her.

"The police are securing the scene. Follow me, I'm going to drive up closer so we're not blocking the driveway."

"Okay." Anxious to do something, anything, she gladly followed Mike to the area in front of the cabin motel. There were two sheriff's vehicles, but even as she arrived, two of the deputies were returning from a path in the woods.

Jillian frowned, wondering why they didn't have Barton in custody. And where were Hawk and Ryker?

"What's going on?" A deputy standing near his vehicle asked.

"We've been instructed by the FBI to clear the area," one of the deputies from the woods replied.

"What do the Feds have to do with this?"

"No idea. But we're out of here."

"Wait, what are you talking about? What happened back there?" Mike protested.

"Listen, this is above our pay grade. You want to argue with a senator and the FBI? Have at it." The deputy didn't so much as give Mike a second glance.

None of this was making any sense. Jillian stayed inside the SUV with Lizzy, watching in confusion as the sheriff's deputies returned to their respective vehicles.

A loud thumping sound had her tightening her grip on the steering wheel. The helicopter! No! Wait! She wanted to scream at the top of her lungs. Had Barton convinced the cops to back off? Was the senator right now taking off with Hawk bound and gagged in the chopper? And what about Ryker? Had he tried to help rescue Hawk? Or was he still hiding somewhere in the woods?

The sound of the helicopter leaving didn't seem to bother the deputies. They didn't waste a second in getting into their respective vehicles and driving back down the winding driveway leading to the highway, giving her the sense that they wanted to distance themselves from whatever had gone down.

Unable to sit still a moment longer, Jillian pushed open her door and jumped out. Her gaze cut to Mike. "What was that about?" She had to shout in order to be heard above the helicopter. "Where's Hawk? And Ryker?"

Mike and Matt exchanged an uneasy glance. "No idea, but sit tight. We'll check it out."

"Maybe one of us should stay back?" Matt suggested.

"No. Both of you go and find them. Hurry!" Jillian felt sick to her stomach, fearing the worst. "Please?"

Mike headed toward the woods, while Matt followed more slowly with Duchess at his side.

She stood, her arms crossed protectively over her chest, staring at the helicopter that moved swiftly across the horizon. Her stomach was in knots at the thought that Senator Barton had Hawk as his prisoner.

She never should have agreed to leave. If not for Lizzy, she wouldn't have. But Hawk had been right to remind her that Lizzy's safety had to be her top priority.

There was a rustling sound from behind her. She frowned, wondering if a deer or some other animal had come out of hiding, or if Ryker had decided to make his presence known.

She turned, her eyes widening in surprise when she saw a man standing there, holding a gun pointed directly at her.

Jillian froze, her heart thumping wildly in her chest.

Not Ryker. A stranger. But not a total stranger—there was something familiar about his facial features.

"Well, if it isn't Mrs. James Wade." The man was dressed all in black, which reminded her of the men who'd chased them through the woods at Hawk's cabin.

"Who are you?" She demanded.

"You don't recognize me? I suppose I should be grateful for that." He took a step toward her and then gestured toward the SUV with the nose of his gun. "Get in."

His facial features suddenly clicked in her mind. She remembered him as the man who'd told her James was dead as well as seeing his face on the computer screen.

Colin Yonkers, the former special ops soldier turned mercenary.

"Now!"

She didn't want to get into the car, but the bite in his tone wasn't easy to ignore. She looked helplessly through the window at Lizzy, wondering if this was how it would end.

No, she refused to give up. Jillian opened the driver's-side door, silently praying for God to provide her the strength and wisdom she needed to save her daughter.

SIXTEEN

Hawk led the way back through the woods toward the cabin motel, stopping abruptly when he came face-to-face with Mike and Matt Callahan.

"What happened?" Mike demanded.

Hawk glanced at Ryker, who shrugged. "Barton covered for us with the deputies and left. Where is Jillian and Lizzy?"

"Waiting in the clearing," Matt answered.

Hawk scowled. "I trusted you to keep them safe."

"She insisted," Mike said wryly. "It was all I could do to make her stay in the SUV with your daughter."

Duchess wheeled around then, growling low in her throat. Matt instantly removed the K-9's leash so as not to hamper the dog's ability to move. "What is it, girl?"

Hawk didn't like the way Duchess was acting, especially when the K-9 instantly turned around and disappeared back the way they'd come. Pushing past Matt, Hawk ran after Duchess.

His vision was growing blurry, but he forced himself to keep going. Something was wrong. Very wrong. The K-9 had picked up on it.

Hawk burst through the trees into the clearing. His

gaze landed on Jillian standing near the driver's-side door of the SUV. There was a man dressed in black standing behind her.

He came to an abrupt halt roughly twenty feet from them when he realized the guy was holding a gun. Duchess stood right in front of Jillian and the gunman, continuing to growl low in her throat.

"Duchess, heel," Matt commanded.

It took a moment for the K-9 to abandon her post. She trotted to Matt's side and sat, ears perked forward as she continued to stare at the gunman.

"Stay back, or I'll kill her," the gunman threatened.

Hawk took a deep breath and let it out, slowly. He recognized the gunman as his old buddy, Colin Yonkers.

For a moment he wondered if the guy was here alone or if other mercenaries were right now hiding in the woods.

"Well, if it isn't my old friend James Wade," Yonkers drawled in a snide tone. "I couldn't believe it when we found out you were still alive."

"I'm sure." Hawk tried to think of a way to get Yonkers away from Jillian. He felt a flash of anger toward Senator Barton. The guy knew Yonkers was guilty but hadn't had him arrested.

And now the former soldier was holding a gun on his wife. Hawk needed to find a way to keep Yonkers focused on him, rather than on Jillian and Lizzy.

From where he stood, he was close enough to the SUV to hear Lizzy crying from inside the SUV.

"It's me you want, Yonkers," Hawk called out, holding his hands up in a gesture of surrender. "Let the woman go. I'm the one you want. It's been that way since Afghanistan, hasn't it?"

"You've been a problem from the very beginning, James," Colin said in a conversational tone. "But it ends here. I want all three of you to drop your weapons. Now!"

Three? Hawk did his best not to react to the realization that one of them hadn't stumbled forward into the clearing, and was still in hiding.

Had to be Ryker.

"Okay, fine." Hawk carefully took the strap of the AK-47, which he'd picked up from the ground after the senator had flown off in his chopper, from around his body and tossed the gun to his left side. The motion sent a shaft of pain up his arm, but he ignored it.

He needed every ounce of his strength and will to get them out of this mess.

Please, Lord, I need You now more than ever. Grant me the strength to protect Jillian, Lizzy and the Callahans.

"The others, too," Yonkers insisted.

Hawk didn't dare look back at Matt and Mike. He kept his gaze focused on the hostile in front of him. He heard the sound of two thuds indicating the Callahan brothers had tossed their weapons aside.

He knew Ryker was armed, but that wouldn't help unless he could figure out how to get Jillian far enough away from Yonkers for Ryker to get a clean shot.

"Take me," Hawk repeated. "She doesn't know anything."

"I'm not so sure about that," Yonkers replied, obviously stalling for time as he planned his next move. Hawk had the impression that the guy had hoped to have Jillian and Lizzy in his custody as hostages before Hawk returned. And that he hadn't realized the Callahans were at the scene as well.

Two small facts in their favor.

"Where's your sister, Olivia?" Hawk asked.

His attempt to divert Colin's attention worked. The former soldier frowned. "What do you mean? Olivia is fine."

"Not so much," Hawk countered. "I was at her place, and she's missing. So is her son, Aaron."

Yonkers looked confused for a moment, then gave his head a little shake. "You're lying. She's fine. I stashed her someplace safe."

"Does your sister know her husband is dead?" Hawk was hoping, praying, that Ryker would get in position, soon. "That I killed him at the cabin?"

The flash of guilt in Yonkers's eyes confirmed that he'd told his sister the truth. Had Olivia blamed Colin for her husband's death? "Shut up!"

Hawk ignored the directive. "You can't kill us all," he pointed out. "You may as well take me and let the others go. Too many dead bodies and the authorities will get suspicious."

"Not if I make it look like an accident," Yonkers countered. "It worked for the plane crash in the mountains."

Hawk wasn't surprised to hear Yonkers knew all about the plane crash over the Appalachian Mountains. Yet Barton seemed to think that the sabotage was someone higher up in the arms-running organization. Like maybe the owners of the mercenary group.

"What, you're planning to stuff all of us in the SUV?" Hawk was determined to keep Yonkers talking. He imagined Ryker was hiding in the woods, planning his next move. "Doubt that will work."

"No, I think the cabin will be better. A Christmas tree fire that got out of control, killing every one of you."

Yonkers gestured with his gun. "You three go inside first, with the dog. One wrong move and I won't hesitate to put a bullet into Mrs. Wade's pretty little head."

Hawk didn't want to go inside the cabin, leaving Jillian and Lizzy with the mercenary. But what choice did he have?

Jillian stared at him with wide, frightened eyes. He could tell she was worried about Lizzy. He wanted to reassure her that they'd find a way out of this mess, but he knew that Ryker wouldn't make his move unless Jillian was out of harm's way.

"We aren't the only ones who know about the gun sales to the insurgents," Hawk said. "We already sent the proof to the authorities." It was a desperate bluff and he knew it. Yet there was always the possibility Yonkers might buy his story.

"If you had, this place would be crawling with Feds. Besides, I was hiding in the woods when the locals left. Now get into the cabin, or she dies." Yonkers lifted his gun closer to the back of Jillian's head.

Feeling as if he were letting her down in the worst way possible, he took a step toward the cabin, his brain frantically searching for a way out.

"Your plan won't work," Jillian abruptly said, breaking her silence. "We don't have a Christmas tree. Killing us in the cabin will never look like an accident."

"A faulty heater, then." Yonkers wasn't daunted by Jillian's comment. "I'll figure out something, now get moving!"

Hawk took another step, when a slight movement in the trees behind Yonkers caught his eye.

Finally! Ryker was in position.

It was now or never. They couldn't risk being held

up in the cabin. The close quarters would only work against them.

He looked directly at Jillian, imploring her to understand what he needed her to do. She returned his stare for a long second. Then she deliberately closed both of her eyes and opened them again. Good. That meant she was in sync with his plan. She had no doubt figured out that Ryker was still out there and could help them. She was willing to do whatever was necessary.

He looked down at the ground, then back up at her. He did it twice and she blinked again, acknowledging the plan.

Time stopped as if the universe was holding its breath, waiting for what would come next.

"Now!" Hawk shouted as he dove to the ground. Duchess let out a series of loud barks, distracting Yonkers.

Jillian hit the ground at the same time Hawk shouted. A sharp crack of gunfire echoed through the clearing.

Yonkers dropped forward, hitting the ground right behind Jillian, the impact from Ryker's well-placed bullet taking him out. Hawk shoved himself upright and ran over to Jillian. After taking a moment to kick Yonkers's gun out of the way, he turned to attend to his wife.

"Are you okay?" He patted her arms and legs, searching for any sign of an injury.

"Fine," she managed. She threw herself into Hawk's embrace as Matt and Mike rushed forward. Duchess stood guard over Yonkers, as if determined to make sure the guy didn't get back up.

He didn't.

"Lizzy," Jillian said in a choked voice. "I don't want her to see Yonkers."

Hawk looked up at Matt, who quickly went around to the other side of the SUV. Matt opened the back passenger door, then deftly unbuckled Lizzy from her car seat. He hauled her into his arms, cradling her close, staying on the opposite side of the SUV from where Yonkers was lying on the ground.

"It's okay, everything is fine," Matt crooned. Duchess came over to his side, apparently understanding that Yonkers was no longer a threat.

Duchess nudged Lizzy's foot with her nose and Lizzy turned her tear-streaked face toward the K-9. "Duchess," she said, holding out her tiny hand toward the animal.

The diversion worked. Hawk helped Jillian to her feet and together gave the mercenary a wide berth as they went over to where Matt waited with Lizzy.

Ryker had come out of the woods and was talking to Mike, no doubt getting the other side of the story that he'd missed while hiding.

"You're sure there isn't anyone lurking around?" Hawk asked.

"I didn't find anyone. That's what took me so long to get around to a spot behind Yonkers. I had to move slowly, to be sure I didn't stumble onto any unpleasant surprises."

Hawk nodded. "Nice timing." Hawk didn't look away from his buddy when Jillian took Lizzy into her arms. "That's twice you bailed me out in a matter of hours."

Under different circumstances, he knew Ryker might have made a smart comeback. But his buddy eyed Jillian and Lizzy, and simply nodded.

"Yes, thank you, Ryker." Jillian's smile was wobbly and she looked as if she might cry. Hawk knew they needed to call this in, and to turn over the evidence they had about the arms dealing to the FBI. He felt certain that with Yonkers gone, the rest of the operation would fall apart.

The danger was finally over.

Jillian collapsed on the sofa inside the cabin, cradling Lizzy close. Her entire body trembled, and even though logically she knew the danger was over, she couldn't seem to stop shaking. It was as if Yonkers still held the gun on her.

If not for God watching over them, she knew this situation would have ended badly. Yonkers had made it clear that he would find a way to kill them all in order to protect his secret.

So many deaths, all to cover up the sale of American guns to the insurgents.

She hoped and prayed Lizzy hadn't seen too much from her car seat. Of if she had, that her daughter was too young to understand.

Duchess followed her to the sofa, as if instinctively knowing that Jillian and Lizzy needed her. Lizzy put a hand on Duchess's silky fur and murmured, "Nice doggie."

"We're safe now, Lizzy," she assured her daughter.

Lizzy nodded and cuddled her teddy bear close.

Hawk stood there watching them for a moment, then pulled out his phone. "I need to call Barton. He needs to help us mitigate the damage from taking down Yonkers. I'm sure it won't be long before the sheriff's deputies return. I'm surprised the owner of this place hasn't called them already."

"Agreed." Ryker lifted a brow. "You better sit down to make the call, Hawk. You're not looking so good."

That caught Jillian's attention. She sent a sharp gaze toward Hawk in time to see him sway a bit before dropping into the closest kitchen chair.

She wondered when he'd taken his last dose of antibiotic. It wasn't easy to shift her daughter off her lap and onto the sofa. Duchess lightly jumped up next to Lizzy, curling up beside the little girl.

Jillian pushed off the sofa and headed toward Hawk. "Where are your antibiotics?"

Hawk shook his head and then turned his attention to his call. "Barton? It's Hawk. Yonkers is dead. He threatened to kill Jillian, so we took him out of commission." Hawk fell silent for a moment. "Yeah, get here as soon as you can. Bring the Feds."

Jillian put her hand on Hawk's arm, gasping at the heat emanating from his skin. He was running a fever. Taking more oral antibiotics weren't going to help.

He needed to get to the hospital.

"Ryker, will you please stay here with Mike?" Jillian asked. "Matt, I'd like you and Duchess to come with me and Lizzy while we take Hawk to the closest hospital. He's burning up with a fever and I'm sure his gunshot wound is infected."

"Not yet," Hawk protested. "I need to wait for Senator Barton."

"Why?" Jillian demanded. "Ryker and Mike can fill Barton in on the details. You can't wait much longer."

Hawk remained stubbornly silent. She sent Ryker an imploring look. "Talk to him, will you?"

Ryker let out a sigh. "Hawk, listen to your wife. We have this under control."

"What about the Blake-Moore group?" Hawk asked,

enunciating the words carefully as if he were having trouble speaking. "They're still out there, somewhere."

Jillian felt a chill snake down her back. "I thought Ryker checked the area for them?"

"Not here," Ryker quickly spoke up. "He just means that the organization is still in business."

It occurred to her then that they still hadn't figured out who had hired the Blake-Moore group. Although, at the moment, she didn't care. Hawk had begun to shiver, despite the burning heat radiating from his skin. "We need to go now. Or call an ambulance." She glared at him. "Your choice."

"No ambulance." The words were a bit slurred and that was enough to scare her almost as much as being held at gunpoint.

Maybe more. Hawk had been so strong, so invincible since the moment he'd saved her from the masked gunmen at her house, that it hurt to see him like this.

"Matt, I need your help." She tried to help Hawk stagger to his feet, but he was far too heavy.

Thankfully, Ryker and Mike stepped up to help. With a man on either side of Hawk, they hauled him to his feet. Jillian went over to the sofa to get Lizzy.

"No! Don't wanna ride in the car!" Lizzy kicked out her feet. "I'm hungry!"

"I know." Jillian felt bad she'd forgotten about providing food for her daughter. So much had happened in what seemed like such a short time. "We'll take some crackers with us in the car. We need to take Daddy to the hospital, okay?"

"Will these work?" Matt pulled a box of saltine crackers from the cupboard.

"Yes, thanks." She wrestled Lizzy back into her coat. "We'll ride with Duchess. Won't that be fun?"

Bringing up the dog worked. Lizzy took the proffered cracker and began to eat as Jillian carried her out to the car. She was horrified at how weak Hawk was in his efforts to get into the vehicle.

"Should I call an ambulance?" She glanced at Matt, indecision crowding her eyes.

"By the time they get here, you could be more than halfway to the hospital." Matt opened the back of the SUV for Duchess. "I say we just go. I'll drive."

She didn't argue, knowing it was best to have her hands free to keep Lizzy happy with crackers. Besides, she was worried about Hawk. They'd put him in the back next to Lizzy.

Matt didn't waste any time in barreling out of the long, winding driveway to the highway. Traffic was light, but since it this late in December, dusk was already beginning to fall although it was barely three thirty in the afternoon.

Twisting in her seat, Jillian looked back at Hawk. He was slumped in the corner, with his eyes closed. Lizzy was munching another cracker, seemingly in a better mood.

"Hurry, Matt," she whispered. "I'm worried about him."

"I know." Matt pressed his foot harder on the accelerator.

The ride seemed to take forever, but it was surprisingly only fifteen minutes before Matt gestured to the blue H sign, indicating the hospital was up ahead. "We're close now."

"Good." Jillian handed Lizzy another cracker, then

leaned back to pat Hawk's knee. "Hawk? Can you hear me? We're almost at the hospital."

Hawk's eyelashes fluttered but he didn't respond. A cold fist of fear clutched her heart.

What if they were too late? What if the infection in Hawk's bloodstream was too far gone?

She couldn't bear the thought of losing Hawk. She needed him. Lizzy needed him.

When Matt pulled up to the front of the entrance marked Emergency, she jumped out and ran inside. "Help! We need help!"

Two staff members wearing scrubs followed her outside. Matt had opened the back door and was trying to support Hawk's weight.

"Get a gurney!"

One of the staff members spun around to head back inside. Jillian hovered near the nurse.

"He suffered a gunshot wound in his left shoulder a few days ago. I'm afraid it's infected."

The nurse barely glanced at her. "He's going into septic shock. We need to get him inside, stat!"

Septic shock? Jillian couldn't believe how Hawk had gotten so sick, so fast. She moved out of the way to make room for the stretcher. With Matt's help, the two hospital staff members were able to get Hawk on the gurney. After securing the straps around his torso, they quickly ran with him inside the emergency department.

Jillian watched them go, then slumped against the SUV and buried her face in her hands.

Dear Lord, please heal Hawk's infection. Don't take him from me to bring him home to You. Not yet. Please? Amen.

SEVENTEEN

The bright overhead lights hurt his eyes and the muted sounds of voices were unintelligible. For a moment he wondered if he were being held prisoner in Afghanistan, because he couldn't understand what the people around him were saying. But then slowly, fragments of conversation began to make sense.

"Give another liter fluid bolus. Has the antibiotic run in yet?"

"Yes, it's in. Second fluid bolus is infusing now. Check out his labs, looks as if he's still a bit acidotic."

"Repeat his basic chem and have it run stat."

"Okay. Should I call upstairs for a bed?"

"No, we need to arrange a transfer to Trinity Medical Center. That bullet wound in his shoulder will need surgical intervention."

"I'll get the Access Center on the phone."

Some of it was gibberish, but Hawk began to realize that he was in the hospital getting treatment for his infected shoulder. And that they were planning to transfer him back to Milwaukee's Trinity Medical Center.

Except he wasn't going anywhere. Not until he knew where his family was.

"Jillian." The word was little more than a dry croak.

"Just relax, Mr. Jacobson, you're doing fine." A hand rested lightly on his right shoulder.

"Jillian." He repeated her name with more force, determined to get an answer. Where were Jillian and Lizzy? He didn't like being separated from them. As much as he trusted Ryker and the Callahans, he couldn't relax until he knew where Jillian and Lizzy were.

Bits and pieces of the most recent events were coming back to him. Primarily Senator Barton taking off in his helicopter, and Yonkers holding Jillian at gunpoint. They way they'd managed to get away from him.

Logically he knew the danger was over.

But he sensed there was more. He kept coming back to the way Barton believed someone higher up was pulling the strings. Who had hired the Blake-Moore group? Someone within the government? Was that higher up? He wondered about General McCann and Major Todd Hayes.

One of them or someone else, but likely the same man who'd sabotaged the plane that killed his teammates.

The nurse moved away and he quickly reached out with his strong hand, grabbing onto her forearm with a firm grip. Whatever they'd given him so far, it seemed to have done the trick. He could feel his strength returning by the minute. "Where's Jillian?"

"Easy now, you're going to dislodge the IV we placed." Her voice was soothing while she tried to wrestle her wrist from his grasp. "Maybe we need to give you something to help the pain and reduce your anxiety."

He instantly let her go. "No. I don't want narcotics or any sedatives. I'll be fine once you tell me exactly where my wife and daughter are."

"I think they're in the waiting room," someone spoke up.

Hawk squinted against the harsh lights, trying to put a face with the voice. "I need to see them. I'm not leaving until I see them."

"I'll see what I can do," the voice promised.

Hawk relaxed and tried to take stock of his situation. His left shoulder still throbbed, but not nearly as badly as before. He didn't feel feverish, either, and assumed the antibiotic they'd spoken about had already begun to fight against the infection. He felt stronger and thought that he could likely get out of there under his own power, if needed.

He didn't remember much of the trip to the hospital. Last thing he remembered, he'd been freezing cold and shivering, his brain feeling as if it were muffled by cotton. Then suddenly he'd awoken here under the bright lights, surrounded by medical personnel.

"Hawk?" Jillian's voice was full of trepidation. He turned his head and tried to see her more clearly. If only they'd shut that stupid light off. It was making his head hurt.

"I'm fine." He managed to drum up a weak smile. He held out his hand, grateful when she clasped it tightly. "Lizzy?"

"She's okay. I left her with Ryker because I wasn't sure how bad you'd look." Jillian stepped closer and he took note of the worried furrows in her brow. "You scared me. I've never seen you so sick."

"No reason to be afraid, Jilly. I've suffered far worse than this." Although he had to admit modern medicine did wonders for helping a guy get over a raging infection. "They want to transfer me to Trinity, but I need to get out of here."

"That's not a good idea," Jillian protested. "You seem better, but you don't realize how bad you were just a couple of short hours ago. Now that we're all safe, I'd rather you get the treatment you need."

The immediate danger was over, but Hawk knew that he wouldn't rest until he'd spoken personally with the FBI about what he knew and what he'd theorized.

"Did Barton show up?"

"I don't know, but Ryker took Matt back to the cabin and just returned a few minutes ago." Jillian glanced around as if she were uncomfortable talking to Hawk in the middle of the emergency department. "They told me I could only stay a few minutes. And I need to get back to Lizzy. Please listen to the doctor."

He didn't want her to leave. He didn't like having her and Lizzy out of his sight. But he nodded. "Stay in the waiting room for a little while yet, okay?"

"We will." She surprised him by leaning down to press a kiss on his cheek. "I'm glad you're better, Hawk."

"Me, too." He ached to kiss her properly, but she was already moving away. A glance up at the IV pole confirmed the fluid the nurse had hung was only a fourth of the way infused.

He decided to wait until the full liter was finished, before getting out of there. The cops would be there soon as gunshot wounds were an automatic report to the police. Even though it had happened days ago, Hawk didn't want to deal with the local law enforcement agencies.

He'd need Barton and his FBI buddy to avoid ending up in jail.

His condition must have stabilized because the bevy of hospital staff around his bedside dwindled and the bright lights were dimmed to a tolerable level. The doctor returned and informed him that Trinity Medical Center was willing to accept him as a transfer and that an ambulance would be there shortly.

It was on the tip of his tongue to refuse the transfer, but then he realized this was his ticket out of there. "I can't afford an ambulance ride. My wife will drive me."

The physician frowned, not liking that answer. "You can't go in a personal vehicle with an IV running."

"Take it out." Hawk kept his tone reasonable. "I'm not riding in an ambulance all the way to Milwaukee. That's a ridiculous waste of money when I have access to a vehicle and someone to drive me."

The doctor reluctantly nodded as if the financial aspect of Hawk's argument made sense. "Fine. But I think someone from the sheriff's department will be here to talk to you first."

Yeah, that wasn't happening. Hawk waited for the doctor to move away, then yanked out the IV, pressing the edge of the sheet over the bleeding wound until it stopped. He swung upright and managed to get off the gurney. Thankfully, they hadn't taken off all his clothes, but his warm leather jacket was nowhere to be seen. Hoping Jillian had it, he moved into the hallway and looked for the waiting room.

"Hey, where are you going?" a nurse asked in a sharp tone.

"Doc said I was accepted at Trinity. My wife is driving me." He didn't wait for her to respond but followed his instincts and managed to find the waiting area.

Jillian had his leather jacket and was sitting with Ryker. Lizzy was between them. He grabbed the jacket and gestured toward the door. "Let's go."

Ryker didn't hesitate. Jillian helped Lizzy with her

coat, then scooped her into his arms. "I'm not happy about this," she muttered.

He ignored her. It wasn't until they were outside and back in the SUV that he relaxed.

"Where to?" Ryker asked as he started the engine.

Good question. "I need to talk to Barton. Where are the Callahans?"

"They're at the cabin motel, working with Barton's men." Ryker glanced at him. "You sure you want to go back there?"

"I think that's the only way we'll put this issue to rest once and for all." He was frustrated that his weakness had sent him to the hospital.

"Ryker, the doctor thinks it's important we get him to Trinity Medical Center as quickly as possible," Jillian said from the back seat.

"Later. Once I've spoken to Barton. I have no doubt I can call him and convince him to return to the cabin motel." Hawk didn't like disappointing Jillian, but she didn't understand what was at stake. Although Yonkers was dead, it didn't mean others weren't involved or weren't already working out a plan to continue selling guns to the insurgents.

"It won't take long to talk to Barton, then we'll head to Milwaukee." Ryker turned onto the highway and glanced back at Jillian. "Trust me, I'll make him go in."

Hawk didn't respond. He respected Ryker enough to know the guy wasn't kidding. He'd hoped to be home with Jillian and Lizzy for Christmas—their first holiday as a family, and maybe that was still a possibility.

A sudden crack echoed through the air. A metallic ping made the SUV jerk as Ryker fought to keep the vehicle on the road. Hawk braced himself with a hand on the dashboard as the scent of gas filled the interior, the fumes adding to his nagging headache.

"What's happening?" Jillian asked in horror.

All Hawk knew was that it wasn't good. Ryker steered the SUV toward the side of the road not far from a densely wooded area, then threw the gearshift into Park.

"Let's go."

Hawk scrambled from the car, then opened the back passenger door for Lizzy, fumbling with the straps to free her from the car seat. Jillian quickly joined him.

They'd barely taken three steps when a spotlight suddenly lit them up brighter than a Christmas tree. Hawk froze, holding Lizzy to his chest and raising a hand against the glare.

"It's been a long time, hasn't it, James?"

He couldn't see but he tried to place the voice. It wasn't familiar, despite the way this guy had addressed him. "Not long enough, obviously," he responded. "Who are you?"

"You don't remember me? I'm crushed." The man stepped forward, but it wasn't until he'd gotten closer that Hawk recognized him.

Former major of the Special Forces unit and current secretary of defense, Todd Hayes.

The man who'd no doubt hired the Blake-Moore group and had been in on the arms deal with Yonkers all along.

Jillian couldn't believe it was happening all over again. She had thought they were safe! That after Yonkers had died, their lives would go back to normal.

But as the man wearing a long winter coat and holding a gun approached casually, she began to realize that they'd never been safe. Not since the moment James had witnessed the gun deal in the Afghan mountains.

"It was you all the time, wasn't it? You were the one Yonkers reported to back in Afghanistan. You knew all about how he was selling guns to the insurgents. In fact, you gave him the order to do so, didn't you?" Hawk subtly shifted Lizzy in his arms. Jillian reached up to take their daughter, who had once again begun to cry in a way that wrenched her heart.

Lizzy had been exposed to far too much danger in the past few days and Jillian wondered how the little girl would manage to cope.

"You should have died in that plane crash." Hayes's voice was laced with annoyance. "If you had, your family would have been safe."

Considering the way her house had been breached by two thugs and her classroom ransacked, Jillian didn't believe him. She was fairly certain that the men with ski masks could have made her death and Lizzy's look like a burglary gone bad, once they had gotten the photos they'd come for.

She wished she'd never made that fateful call to Fort Bragg about the envelope from James.

"Yeah, right." Hawk's sarcastic tone reflected her feelings. "So now what? You're going to kill us all right here at the side of the road?"

"It would have helped if you'd crashed," Hayes drawled. "But we can work with it."

We? She shivered, imagining there were more men dressed in black, moving through the woods right now. Was it possible that Hayes had brought more members of the Blake-Moore group with him? That this time, they wouldn't have a chance to escape?

"This close to the hospital? Better think again," Hawk shot back.

She realized Hawk was right. Ryker hadn't gotten far from the hospital when the shot had rung out, striking their gas tank. And who'd fired the shot anyway? Not Hayes but one of his minions.

Turning slightly to the right, she verified the lights from the hospital were within view.

So close, yet so far. If anyone at the hospital had heard the gunshot, there was no indication that they'd noticed. Or bothered to do anything about it.

She could feel Ryker coming up on her right side, as if planning to jump in front of her if Hayes started shooting. Sensing his presence didn't make her feel better. She wished he'd found a way to hide in the woods. Unfortunately, the spotlight had made that impossible.

Also, the goons were likely hiding in the woods, waiting for their chance to shoot.

And suddenly she was fed up with everything. "You won't get away with this," she shouted loud enough to startle Lizzy. "Senator Barton knows all about you."

Hayes threw back his head and laughed. Jillian felt her cheeks flush with fury. What was so funny?

"Barton has already been silenced and I've given orders for his men not to go anywhere near the cabin motel where you so rudely took out my main contact, Colin Yonkers." All hint of humor abruptly vacated his voice. "Enough. It's time for you to get back inside the vehicle."

Jillian inwardly reeled at his words. Barton had been silenced? The men hadn't gone to the cabin motel? Where were the Callahans?

She felt Hawk and Ryker go tense on either side of her

and knew they were about to make some sort of drastic last-minute move.

Only this time, there was no easy way to get away. Not if there were men hiding in the woods around them.

"Okay, we're getting into the vehicle." Once again she blurted out her thoughts without taking the time to think it through.

"Jilly," Hawk warned in a low voice.

But then the shrill wail of sirens split the air. Jillian couldn't help taking a quick glance down the highway in the direction they'd been headed.

Twin red and blue flashing lights were fast approaching. She stood frozen, wondering if help was on the way or if the secretary of defense had somehow gotten the cops on his side, as well?

EIGHTEEN

About time, Hawk thought. The wailing sirens indicated the local authorities were on the way. He'd been counting on the fact that the ER doctor had called the police to report his gunshot wound, and likely his recent escape. And here they were, just in the nick of time.

The spotlight went dark, and it took a long moment for his eyes to adjust to the instant darkness. He heard the scrape of footsteps on asphalt.

"We can't let him get away!" Hawk glanced toward Ryker, but the former special ops soldier didn't move.

"We don't know how many men he has with him." Ryker gently brushed past Jillian. "Stay with your family. I'll talk to the cops."

The sound of a car engine rumbling to life made Hawk want to rush after Hayes to stop him. But he wasn't armed. And Ryker was right. They knew for sure Hayes wasn't alone, having more than enough mercenaries at his disposal.

But then there was another SUV coming from the opposite direction from the local deputies. Hawk tensed, fearing the worst.

The oncoming SUV rammed directly into Hayes's vehicle. Two men instantly came out of the car, followed by a K-9.

The Callahans.

"Put your hands where I can see them!" Mike shouted. Even from where they stood, Hawk could hear Duchess growling.

"You don't know who you're messing with, son!" Hawk could hear the undertone of fear in Hayes's voice. "I'm the Secretary of Defense for the United States of America!"

"You're also a lying, gun-selling criminal," Mike retorted. "Keep your hands where I can see them, and your buddy in the driver's seat, too, or I'll shoot first and ask questions later."

"You'll pay for this!" Desperation leached from Hayes. "You can't arrest me! Who do you think you are?"

While Mike held his gun pointed at Hayes, Matt opened the passenger-side door and roughly yanked Hayes out. Duchess continued to growl, encouraging Hayes to comply. Matt turned him face first toward the SUV and slapped cuffs around his wrists.

The driver didn't put up a fight, either, but stood stoic and silent as Matt cuffed him, as well.

Two sheriff's department vehicles pulled to a stop near the group of SUVs. Four armed deputies emerged, holding their guns at the ready.

"Which one of you is Milwaukee County Deputy Mike Callahan?"

"Over here," Mike called, without turning from the two men he still held in the crosshairs of his weapon. "We have two men in custody here, but be on alert, as there could be more."

"He's right. Someone fired at our car, hitting the gas

tank," Ryker added. "Had to be from a rifle. If there's no such weapon in the car with them, then someone in the woods has it."

Hawk knew that if there were any mercenaries from the Blake-Moore group still hiding in the woods, they'd be long gone. Mercs were always ready to cut and run in order to save their own skin. It burned to know they wouldn't all be brought to justice.

Although if he had his way, the Blake-Moore group would never be hired by anyone within the US government, ever again.

"Release me this instant!" Hayes shouted. "I'm the secretary of defense! I'm the one who was trying to arrest these men for treason!"

"Save it," one of the deputies replied. "We already heard from the FBI. Special Agent in Charge Dennis Ludwig informed us that they recently caught a man who attempted to kill Senator Barton. Seems he worked for you, Hayes, and spilled his guts to save himself. The Feds contacted us and requested we return to the cabin motel."

Hawk's mind spun at the recent turn of events. It was surreal that events at the highest level of the government had spilled over into small-town Wisconsin.

Because of him.

"I have a photo that shows Colin Yonkers selling weapons to the insurgents in Afghanistan," he offered. "Unfortunately, Yonkers is dead, but he worked for the Blake-Moore mercenary group. I think you'll find Hayes hired them to do his dirty work, including shooting me." He put a hand up to rub his injured shoulder.

"I have the photo and your laptop computer. I've heard parts of the story, but we'll need you to come with us so we can hear it all from the beginning." The deputy who'd called to Mike gestured with his hand. "We'll transport Hayes and his driver to jail, too. The Feds are coming in to pick them up."

"No!" Hayes let out a strangled cry and made a move as if to run. Duchess clamped her jaw around his ankle, preventing him from going anywhere.

"Idiot," Ryker muttered.

"What about us?" Jillian asked, speaking for the first time since her impulsive comments about Barton.

Hawk wanted nothing more than to tell her she could go home, but her house was a mess and he still didn't feel good about having her out of his sight. "You'll come with us," he assured her. "Hopefully it won't take too long."

"All right," she agreed with a weary sigh.

He was wrong. Upon entering the sheriff's department headquarters, they were taken to separate rooms. Ryker in one, Hawk in another, and Jillian and Lizzy in a third.

Hawk did his best to start the story at the beginning, but Deputy Greg Ashton, the one who apparently knew Mike, kept interrupting.

When his stomach rumbled with hunger, Deputy Ashton brought him something from the vending machine, but Hawk insisted that he provide food and water to Jillian and Lizzy.

"They're being well taken care of," Ashton assured him, plunking a bag of chips and a bottle of water in front of him. "So you and Tillman shot two of Senator Barton's men, but he covered for you?"

"Yes." Hawk picked up the story, and after another hour, finally finished with how their SUV had been fired upon outside the hospital by Hayes and his men. "I'm telling you, the Blake-Moore group is involved in this up to their beady little eyeballs."

"Yeah, I've been thinking the same thing." Ashton looked down at the pages of scribbled notes on the yellow legal pad in front of him. "Anything else?"

"I don't think so." He'd covered everything, starting with the plane crash that had killed his teammates, and Jillian's phone call to Fort Bragg, which had resulted in the break-in at Jillian's house and Brookland Elementary. He hadn't left out a single detail and hoped he wouldn't be held as an accessory to murder as a result of Yonkers's death.

"Okay, stay here for a minute. I need to talk to my team." Deputy Ashton rose to his feet.

"We only shot at Yonkers because he threatened to kill Jillian," Hawk said in a low voice. "It was him or her. She and Lizzy are the true innocents in all of this."

Ashton stopped at the door. "I believe you, but I need to make sure Tillman's story matches yours. If it does, then I think we'll be okay."

After Ashton disappeared from the room, Hawk slumped in his seat, exhaustion weighing him down. He desperately wanted to see Jillian and Lizzy, to make sure they were both okay.

Thinking of the harm he'd brought to them filled him with shame and self-loathing. He never, ever should have mailed those photos to her. He'd dragged his wife and daughter into harm's way, not just once, but over and over again.

Would things have been different if he'd taken the stupid ambulance to Milwaukee? Probably.

He didn't deserve to have a wife and child in his life. Now that the Feds were involved, Hayes was in custody and the Blake-Moore group was under scrutiny, he felt certain the danger was over. For real, this time.

Maybe he'd give Jillian and Lizzy his house to use temporarily, until hers was repaired. He'd need to return to the hospital sooner than later, anyway. He'd pay for the damage to her home, then move on, giving her the freedom and safety she deserved.

Jillian had refused to allow Lizzy to eat a bunch of junk food from the vending machines, so one of the helpful deputies who had a child of his own had run out to get chicken fingers from a local fast-food restaurant. It wasn't great, but slightly better than chips and cookies.

Lizzy was better now that they were inside, surrounded by men wearing uniforms and badges, but she was clearly getting bored.

"Where's Daddy?" she asked for the third time.

"He'll be here soon." Jillian knew her smile was brittle. She was tired of waiting for the deputies to finish with Ryker and Hawk. Especially since she knew Hawk needed to get back to the hospital.

The Callahan brothers had been there for a while but had left when the FBI agents arrived. She assumed they were walking the agents through the various crime scenes.

"I wanna go home," Lizzy whined.

"I know, sweetie. Me, too." Jillian caught sight of Deputy Ashton coming out of the room where she knew Hawk was seated. Her questioning session hadn't taken nearly as long, and she was becoming concerned with the amount of time they'd spent with Hawk and Ryker.

Especially Hawk.

"Mrs. Jacobson?"

She didn't bother to correct the deputy. At this point, she felt like she was Mrs. Jacobson more so than Mrs. Wade. Her life with James was a long time ago,

She was with Hawk now.

"Yes?" She summoned a smile. "Are we free to go?"

"You are. I've validated that Ryker's story mirrors your husband's."

Of course it did. Hawk and Ryker joined her in the office and she looked at her husband with concern. "Hawk? Are you okay?" Jillian shifted Lizzy in her arms, bone-weary from carrying the little girl.

"Fine." He didn't quite meet her eyes. "Let's get out of here."

She was having trouble gauging his mood. "I'm taking you straight to Trinity Medical Center."

To her surprise, he didn't argue. "Ryker, we need a set of wheels."

She blinked, having completely forgotten about the hole in the gas tank.

"Mike Callahan is letting us borrow his vehicle, and he already put Lizzy's car seat inside," Ryker said.

Jillian walked between the men out into the cold December air. "How will Mike and Matt get home?"

"One of the deputies offered them a lift. Besides, they're still talking to the Feds." Ryker opened the door for her and she gratefully set Lizzy inside.

No one spoke during the long trip to Milwaukee. Jillian sensed Hawk was upset about something, but he insisted he was fine.

At the hospital, Hawk dug a key out of his pocket and handed it to her. "Ryker will take you to my place. Yours needs a bit of repair work."

"I'm not leaving," she protested, although Lizzy's eyelids were drooping with exhaustion.

"You are. Lizzy needs to rest." Hawk didn't reach out to touch her or even hug her. "Take care, Jillian."

His words held a note of finality that made her frown. But Hawk was already making his way inside the brightly lit emergency department. She knew he was safe there, but leaving him felt as if she were cutting off her own arm.

She didn't like it, not one bit. If not for Lizzy, she'd stay with him all night.

"Come on," Ryker said. "I'll take you home."

Home was where Hawk was, but she nodded. Lizzy needed a good night's sleep. But first thing in the morning, she'd be back. And no matter what Hawk said, she wasn't going to leave again.

Not until he was able to come home with her, hopefully in time for Christmas.

Hawk felt much better by the following morning, thanks to more fluids and antibiotics. The hospital staff wasn't happy with him, so he tried to be a model patient.

The surgeon, Dr. Cramer, came in early to poke and prod his injured shoulder. "Could be worse. Can't do much until the infection is cleared out."

"So I can get out of here?"

"What, big plans for Christmas?" Dr. Cramer asked.

Hawk belatedly realized today was Christmas Eve. So much had happened over the past five days that he'd lost track of time.

"Something like that." He shifted in the uncomfortable hospital bed. "It's crazy to just sit here for IV antibiotics."

"They saved your life," Dr. Cramer pointed out. "Sorry, but it's not just the antibiotics, but regular dressing changes."

"Come on, it wasn't that bad," Hawk protested.

"Frankly, I expected worse." Cramer logged into the computer and peered thoughtfully at the screen. "You stay until noon to get another dose of antibiotics and you can return home for two days. I'll expect you back on the day after Christmas."

That wasn't exactly part of his plan, but Hawk wasn't about to argue. "Thanks."

"You can thank me by doing regular dressing changes and taking your antibiotics as ordered." Cramer logged off the computer and left the room.

Hawk dozed a bit but woke up when he heard Lizzy's voice. "Daddy? Are you all better now?"

Daddy? Hawk opened his eyes to find his beautiful daughter standing beside his bed, looking fresh from a bath and wearing clean clothes. She still had the ragged teddy bear that she'd managed to hold on to from the night he'd pulled her out from beneath her bed. "I'm fine, Lizzy." His gaze lifted to meet Jillian's. She also looked better for having had a good night's sleep, a shower and clean clothes. Her beauty was enough to make his heart squeeze painfully in his chest.

"I heard you're going to be given a few days off for good behavior," Jillian joked.

He nodded and pushed himself upright. "I'm surprised to see you here."

She lifted a brow. "Why? You had to know we'd come visit."

He wasn't sure how to respond. He looked past her at the door leading to the hallway. "Is Ryker with you?"

"He dropped us off," Jillian informed him. "He was up early, working on putting my house back in order."

A flash of jealousy hit hard. If anyone should be helping, it should be him. The destruction of her property was his fault, not Ryker's. "I'll help as soon as we leave."

Jillian rolled her eyes. "Keep saying stuff like that and they won't let you go. You're supposed to be recuperating, not working."

"Here. I think you need teddy more than me." Lizzy shoved her favorite stuffed animal in the crook of his arm. The simple gesture made his eyes sting with tears.

"That's nice of you to share teddy with Daddy," Jillian said with a smile.

"She doesn't have to," he started to say, but Jillian silenced him with a stern look.

"Sharing is a nice trait for children to learn, the earlier the better."

Lizzy found the buttons on the electric bed and made the head begin to rise.

"No, Lizzy," Jillian gently scolded. "Behave or Daddy won't be able to come home with us."

Daddy? Home with them? He tried to think of something to say. "Jilly, there's no reason to rush into anything. We have plenty of time to sort things out."

"What's to sort out?" She pulled the Belle doll out of the purse on her shoulder and offered it to Lizzy. "Why don't you play for a bit, okay?"

"Okay." Lizzy took the doll and went over to the recliner chair in the corner of the room.

"It's her favorite," Jillian offered with a smile. "Because it was a gift from you."

Hawk cleared his throat. "She knows I'm her father?"

"Yes. I blurted it out when you got so sick." Jillian

sat on the edge of Hawk's bed. "I was afraid we were going to lose you."

Her words were a balm against his wounded soul. Dredging up every ounce of strength he possessed, he did his best to give her an out. "There's no need to change anything between us, Jillian. The danger is over. You can go back to your place and I'll go to mine."

Her brow furrowed. "Is that your way of telling me you don't care about me, about us, anymore?"

"No!" He couldn't lie, not about this. "You don't understand. I'm trying to set you free. You didn't ask to be mixed up with someone like me."

"Yes, I did," Jillian corrected softly. She placed her hand on the center of his chest, the warmth radiating through his flimsy hospital gown. The modest diamond engagement ring he'd given her five years ago glittered on the third finger of her left hand. "I married you, Hawk. For better or worse. In sickness and in health. Forsaking all others, for as long as we both shall live."

The way she recited their wedding vows while wearing his ring humbled him. And instantly his resolve broke into tiny bits and scattered with the wind.

"I love you, Jillian. I've always loved you."

"I love you, too." She bent down and gave him a long kiss. "You're Hawk to me, now, but the core of you is still James. Crazy as it sounds, I love both of you."

"Does that mean you're willing to become Mrs. Hawk Jacobson?" It was meant to be a joke, but her expression was serious as she nodded.

"Yes, absolutely. But you should know that things are different now. I'm a schoolteacher and love my job. I'm not going to sit home every night waiting for you to get home from work."

"I wouldn't ask you to." Hawk knew that she was right, that things were different now.

Yet somehow, they were also the same.

"Then let me be the first to welcome you home, Hawk." Jillian kissed him again and he held her close, reveling in his good fortune.

Home. Hawk was forced to blink back the sting of tears. He'd never allowed himself to consider the fact that he'd have the chance to return home to be with his family.

"Merry Christmas, Jillian," he whispered.

"Merry Christmas, Hawk," she whispered back.

They wouldn't have gifts or decorations, or presents under the tree, but they'd be together as they celebrated the day Jesus was born.

And that was all that mattered.

* * * * *

If you enjoyed this book, don't miss these other stories from Laura Scott:

Shielding His Christmas Witness
The Only Witness
Christmas Amnesia
Shattered Lullaby
Primary Suspect
Protecting His Secret Son

Available now from Love Inspired Suspense!

Find more great reads at
www.LoveInspired.com

Dear Reader,

I hope you've enjoyed Hawk and Jillian's story, *Soldier's Christmas Secrets*. Many of you asked for Hawk to find his own happy ending, and frankly, I wasn't quite willing to give up the Callahans, either.

I have the utmost respect for all of those who serve our country, and I hope you give this new miniseries, Justice Seekers, a try.

Please take a moment to leave a review; reviews are very important for authors. Also know I love hearing from my readers. I can be found through my website at *www.laurascottbooks.com*, through Facebook at Laura Scott Author and on Twitter @Laurascottbooks. If you're interested in when Ryker's story will be available, join my newsletter through my website. That's where I announce new releases, and I offer a free novella that is not for sale anywhere else, to all newsletter subscribers.

Until next time,
Laura Scott

Get 4 FREE REWARDS!

We'll send you 2 FREE Books plus 2 FREE Mystery Gifts.

Love Inspired® Suspense books feature Christian characters facing challenges to their faith... and lives.

FREE Value Over **$20**

Bryce Kingsley bolted toward the opening of the deserted mill and stepped inside, keeping one hand on the weapon at his side. "Jade?"

"Back here." Her voice reached him, sounding weak, shaky.

He hurried to her, keeping an eye on the surrounding area. Bryce rounded the end of the spindle row to see Jade on the floor, holding her head. Blood smeared a short path down her cheek. "You're hurt!" For a moment, she simply stared up at him, complete shock written across her features. "Jade? Hello?"

She blinked. "Bryce?"

"Hi." He glanced over his shoulder, then swung the beam of the flashlight over the rest of the interior.

"You're here?"

"Yeah. This wasn't exactly the way I wanted to let you know I was coming home, but—"

"What are you doing here?"

"Can we discuss that later? Let's focus on you and the fact you're bleeding from a head wound."

"I…I'm all right."

"Did you get a look at who hit you?"

"No."

A car door slammed. Blue lights whirled through the broken windows and bounced off the concrete-and-brick walls. Bryce helped her to her feet. "Let's get that head looked at."

"Wait." He could see her pulling herself together, the shock of his appearance fading. "I need to take a look at something."

He frowned. "Okay." She went to the old trunk next to the wall. "What is it?"

"The person who hit me was very interested in whatever was over here."

Bryce nodded to the shovel and disturbed dirt in front of the trunk. "Looks like he was trying to dig something up."

"What does this look like to you?"

"Looks like someone's been digging."

"Yes, but why? What could they possibly be looking for out here?"

"Who knows?" Bryce studied the pile of dirt and the bricks. "Actually, I don't think they were looking for anything. I think they were in the middle of *burying* something."

Don't miss
Holiday Homecoming Secrets *by Lynette Eason,*
available December 2019 wherever
Love Inspired® Suspense *books and ebooks are sold.*

LoveInspired.com